The Goddess of Revenge

LUCIA CATHERINE

Acknowledgments

I want to take a moment to thank my readers and my team, a few people close to me that allowed me to vent and bounce ideas and thoughts. Lori DeVries, Maria Picozzi, Terry Hammoutene, Wanda Osepowicz and Cathy Mesaric-Bartlett. Last but definitely not least, my dear friend and editor, Joy Houp. Your belief in me means the world. My amazing cover designer, Dawne Dominque of dusktildawndesigns. A special shout out to my BFF Heidi Lichtner, who not only supports me, but listens to me ramble about stories that randomly pop into my head.

Thank you to the readers and my author friends, who believe in me, and stick with me when I am incapable of believing in myself. You have always shined the light I needed to continue.

Much Love,
   Lucia
   XXXO

Courage is not the absence of fear, but rather the judgment that something else is more important than fear. – Ambrose Redmoon

To those who have suffered or are still suffering from domestic abuse. You are strong. I hear you. I see you. You are loved and have the courage to leave and heal. Blessings.

Prologue

The monster slept. At any moment now, his breathing will stop. I slowly increased the dosage of his muscle relaxers this evening. Two pills crushed in his liquor at dinner, two more while he watched the game. Donovan took the last one himself at bedtime. He claimed he needed them for pain but didn't know pain; he has caused me pain repeatedly. Cracked ribs, broken nose, a fractured arm, teeth knocked out, lacerations on my head, fluid on my knees, concussions, even comas. All because of his temper and the dissatisfaction with his life. I'm done. It's over. I can't really take anymore. The abuse stops tonight.

Donovan is a vicious and vile man. Every single day, he beat and tortured me. My support group protected me in the hospital when no one else could. They unwittingly provided me with the resources to end his reign of terror.

The restraining orders hadn't kept him from hurting me. I'm a daughter, a wife, a mother, a friend, and a spiritual woman. I am a killer.

My name is Andressa, and this is the story of how I overcame an abusive situation. It's quite unconventional and I don't advise anyone to do what I did. I pray for my soul every day as I live in darkness.

One

SENIOR YEAR OF COLLEGE ...

The excitement on the field was palpable during the last football game of the season. Students stomping on the metal bleachers, cheerleaders chanting and dancing, doing flips. The last game of the season, the coach promised to pull Donovan off the bench and into the game. He talked about it for days. The seats vibrated with excitement, almost like an electrical current zipped through the bleachers.

Halftime came and went when Donovan was finally called into the game. I screamed so loudly my throat was raw.

During a play, he took a full body hit from the opposing team's player and he went down with a thud. The few beats of silence were deafening, then came the gasps and panic. Especially from our friends. The medics rushed onto the field and in seconds, they slid him onto a gurney and rushed away. Moments later, we heard the telltale signs of rescue. The sirens permeated the field. I hurried to the locker room area where the coach reported which hospital the EMTs would take him to. Brandie, Donovan's oldest and best friend, drove me to the hospital. Brandie was a cute little blond with bright blue eyes and a petite figure and was just as sweet as she looked. Raised together, Brandie and Donovan became devoted friends from the time when they were toddlers. I liked her from the moment I'd met her. We often enjoyed nights out with her, and she was in a few of my classes.

It was at the hospital that I met Donovan's parents for the first time. They were kind but aloof. Donovan assured me it wasn't me, that they were like that all the time. I overheard his mother speaking with Brandie. His mother told her I was a beautiful girl, and she hoped I was kind to her son. Brandie confirmed that my beauty was both inside and outside. My face flushed at the compliments. I had my father's thick mahogany hair, and my mother's bright green eyes. My eyelashes were full and long. I rarely needed mascara. My body was curvy but at the best weight for my height. Running with the track team helped me stay in shape. I loved being part of the team. I also worked out in the college gym for strength training. They told us he tore his ACL and injured tendons in his kneecap, ending his football career. Forever . He was released from the hospital after surgery on his knee. His personality changed after his injury. He was sad, and I think that's why I agreed to marry him and move to Texas with him.

Three months later, we eloped, just a few days before graduation and prepared to leave for Texas.

I did one last sweep of my dorm room, ensuring I left nothing behind. I turned toward my suitcase and the box of personal items I would take with me. The room looked barren, sad actually. We made our way from Florida to Texas in Donovan's sports car. It was loud but the bright red car was fun. Graduation was over and we were married! My parents weren't happy.

Donovan was every girl's dream date, a football player, strong and handsome. He chose me, this cute baby-faced guy.

His almost jet-black hair and eyes like chocolate orbs against fair skin made him a favorite among the cheerleaders. At the time, I didn't know those dark eyes held terrifying secrets or when enraged, his brown eyes turned black and sinister. He squinted as his teeth clenched. The beginning. A beginning I didn't expect. We attended the University of Central Florida together. Built in a circle and pedestrian-friendly, the college was near Disney. I worked part time in a souvenir shop, where I met Donovan for the first time, at the end of sophomore year. We started on the same day and did our training together. He'd told me recently that his family was wealthy and in the oil business. His father insisted he worked while in college as he had. When we began dating, he told me he thought I was beautiful and wanted to be mine. Me, the person who I thought was just ordinary in looks, and yet he found me attractive and sexy.

I chose the Social Work Program with a minor in Poverty Studies and Social Justice. I loved helping people and was fortunate to have an education and a potential career. Donovan's injury made football impossible for him. He joined his father's oil business, detesting it and constantly bragging about his potential as a football player.

The car's loud exhaust system alerted me that Donovan was approaching the building. I pulled my suitcase while carrying the box. Donovan jumped out and smiled. "You did good. You got rid of a lot!"

"Yep, just my clothes and a few personal items in the box." I had my purse and a change of clothes in my backpack. I watched as Donovan maneuvered the box onto the tight back seat. My suitcase, he shoved next to his bags inside the trunk. A few minutes later, we left the college grounds for the last time.

My tanned legs bounced in excitement. Donovan wore a smile on his face as we entered the interstate. He talked a lot about Texas the last two years and mentioned the sights he wanted to show me. He mentioned the apartment he rented for us in Clayton Heights, a small town outside of San Antonio. Achingly too far from my parents and my brothers. Donovan loved everything about his home state. The culture was in his blood. He claimed Texas flowed through him. Once, I asked him why and he told me, primarily, it was the people. Texans were diverse and welcomed everyone. The people were polite, and he loved the food and shared the love of football. He further explained the canyons, islands, valleys, the hills, mountains, plains, and plateaus. He made it sound so enchanting.

We stopped our first night at a hotel and made love before falling into an exhausted sleep.

I was fond of the hot weather, but Donovan had a problem with the humidity, something he didn't mention when he talked about his life in Texas or our stay in Florida. I knew he had a short fuse during the time we dated, but he'd never hurt me physically. Donovan would squeeze my arm or grasp me too tight when annoyed. Once he pinched my arm to stop me from speaking during a conversation with friends. Sometimes he'd say hurtful comments or ignore me for days, but eventually, he returned to being the sweet guy with whom I lost my innocence. The sex was okay, but what did I have to compare it? I was a virgin when we met, and he was the only one that I let touch me intimately. Of course, coming from a strong religious background, I never told my parents or my two brothers. Even though times were different, and women experimented with their sexuality. My parents ingrained it in me to save myself for my husband.

My in-laws were okay, I guess, kind of reserved. Their world revolved around Donovan. I think they expected him to marry a debutante, but he arrived with me, the dark-haired girl from New York. The granddaughter of immigrants from South America. I'd always felt invisible to them. It was still Donovan's car, Donovan's apartment, Donovan's wife. Umm...I had a name. Maybe had he eased me into marriage after an engagement, he might have offered a glimpse into who he really was. Donovan's attitude changed as soon as we arrived in Texas. He didn't approve of the cramped apartment he could afford on his salary, and he prohibited me from working, demanding to be the sole breadwinner. I was to stay home and have babies. The situation left me in a state of shock.

Two

The first bruise came when I suggested I should get a job to get us into a better apartment. Donovan had come home and complained about the gloomy matchbox we lived in, as he did every night.

"Donovan, why don't I get a job and perhaps we could get an apartment you'd like better? Perhaps closer to work?" I asked.

Donovan stalked into the kitchen where I'd been preparing dinner, grabbed my arm, and turned me around to face him, and backhanded me across the face. I was stunned. No one in my life had ever touched me in anger, not my parents, not anyone!

"Because stupid bitch, I'll make money in this house. I'm the man, that's why!" Donovan said through gritted teeth. His face was a mask of something I'd never witnessed before. Rage.

I ran into the bathroom and remained inside until he went to bed. I slept on the sofa, not wanting to be near him. When I woke, the apartment was empty. Who could I tell? My parents? My brothers? Upset them over this stupid decision that I'd made?

One Saturday, he went through my nightstand and found my

transcript. When he asked me what my GPA was, I lied and quoted the same as his, not to make him feel bad. Donovan struggled with academics. I often studied with him so he could pass and stay with the team.

He waited until his friends came over for drinks that night when he began calling me names, like dumbass and a genius wanna be. He went on and on and not one person stopped him. I sat there seething internally. We didn't speak for the remainder of the evening. After his friends left, I went to bed.

Sunday morning, I was meeting his mom for brunch; she was picking me up since Donovan wouldn't let me use his car. I dressed in one of my few sundresses, this one emerald green, and I paired it with a pair of taupe sandals. It was one of Donovan's favorite outfits. When I stepped from the bedroom, he was watching the small TV in the living area. His gaze fixed on me as he approached. He smelled my perfume, stepped back, unzipped, and exposed himself and covered my dress and shoes in his urine. He sneered, "I'm marking you, like the dog that you are." Donovan's face twisted into a scowl, and he hissed, "Don't move and put your arms at your side." He punched me, his hand curled into a tight fist landing to the side of my head. I reached up to protect my head when he ripped my arms away. He pushed me into the wall as if possessed and grabbed my hair and said, "You are not leaving the house looking like that."

"Like what?" I cried.

"A whore." My sleeveless dress showed nothing but my arms and legs. The hemline fell to my knees. There was no way anyone could deem an ordinary sundress like the one I wore anything but classy. I didn't show off my assets. It wasn't who I was or how I dressed.

"Your mom will be here any minute and I now have to shower and change." I hoped he'd relent knowing his mother was coming and would see what he did to me. His lips in a thin line, he reached for his cell phone and called her.

"Mom, Andressa needs to cancel. The poor girl fell and isn't feeling well. I'm sure next Sunday is fine. I put her to bed with an icepack."

Standing there with a pounding headache, stinking of urine. I turned and went into the bathroom to shower and tossed my clothes into the laundry bag. I stepped into the bedroom, wrapped in a towel, and changed when I heard him flip the lock from the outside. The lock was there when we moved in, although we never used it. Pulling on the doorknob, it wouldn't budge. I yelled and cried. My phone was in my purse. I hadn't eaten anything yet and plopped into the center of the bed and cried. Eventually I pulled my journal from my nightstand and wrote. I held nothing back. Journaling was cathartic, I could share what my voice couldn't.

Come late afternoon, I was in a panic. I had to pee. Donovan wasn't home, and he locked me in with nothing. I found a zip-lock bag with makeup sponges and used it. Is this what my life had come to?

Once his true self emerged, Donovan spiraled out of control. Nothing held him back. He spoke with his hands and his feet, and he used them often. Punches. Kicks. Elbows. I constantly wore bruises as though they were normal. Now I'm broken; afraid to speak, not knowing which word will set him off.

I was often "punished" and locked in the bedroom whenever Donovan had a date. He thought I was stupid, but I knew. I prepared the closet for the next time, with empty jars, a shoebox filled with protein bars and another with water bottles and ear buds. I hid books and magazines I borrowed from the building's library downstairs. While Donovan would be in the apartment with the flavor of the week, he kept me locked in the bedroom.

Donovan became a mean-spirited person. Perhaps he always was. It was almost like, now we were married, he no longer hid his true self. He continued to raise his hands to me, often leaving marks that left me housebound in embarrassment. He called me vile names, cheated on me, and threw it in my face. I was thankful; at least I didn't have to have sex often with him.

I wondered how I didn't realize this part of Donovan existed. What did I miss about his personality? Was it my upbringing? The sheltered youngest of three, with two older brothers, who protected me. My grandparents immigrated to the United States from Brazil when they were newlyweds and settled in New York City to live the American dream. They struggled yet opened their grocery store and raised four hard-working children, my dad being the eldest of the four. My parents now run the business and have added four additional stores.

Shame was my life and the motivator to not tell anyone. He threatened me with death enough and I believed he was capable of doing it.

As if life couldn't get any worse, he began checking my emails and scanning my phone. The names he called me were vicious. It was no longer you're fat or thick. I was now called a cunt, whore, slut. His presence oppressed me. I always felt it, even when he wasn't there.

I didn't want to be this weak person, yet I feared answering back. The beatings were almost daily, and he never once apologized or said it wouldn't happen again. I never felt such hate, nor did I hate or wish death upon someone as much as I did him.

One night, after he complained his steak was tough, I muttered I didn't butcher the cow. The steak had been marinating all day. The same kind I bought him every week. I blurted, "Look, Donovan, it's clear you hate me. Let's just divorce and you can sleep with whomever you want. I'll go home."

He snorted, "Divorce? No fucking way. I'll beat you into being the dutiful wife I need." He laughed like a maniac and turned to me. "I will kill you, your sanctimonious parents, those wrinkled old immigrants you so worship, and your pussy brothers before I allow you to divorce me."

One time when he had to explain his bruised knuckles at work, he found weapons to use. Hammers, belts, the security bar in the sliding doors, slammed my head into walls, doors. Threatened me with knives from the block in the kitchen. When I stopped sleeping in bed with him, he dragged me by my hair inside and raped me by knife point. I begged for him to kill me. Anything to be put out of this miserable life. I'm on guard 24/7. I'm sleep deprived. Deep breath in. Exhale. Repeat.

Neighbors often called the police. I tried restraining orders, leaving him, but he always found me and forced me back with threats. My parents, my friends, I believed he could do serious harm if he could hurt me this badly. Why not others? The police never enforced the restraining orders. I joined a support group for comfort and attended meetings to listen and enjoy the group's warmth. I could only take part when Donovan was out for the evening or early morning meetings while he worked. It surprised me to learn how many women were abused in the community.

For three years, I suffered at Donovan's hands. I'd lost count of the number of broken bones, countless stitches, bruises, and concussions. The month before his death, I was in a coma because he'd hit the back of my head with a cast-iron skillet. My friends from the support group sat by my side, twenty-four hours a day, and refused to allow admittance to Donovan or his family. When I woke, they'd offered me safe places to live. The group banned him from my hospital room. I'd never have a peaceful day; Donovan's beatings were relentless. It came to me in a dream about what I needed to do. What had to happen for me to be safe.

I've had so many hospital stays, none because Donovan called an ambulance. It was always the neighbors. Particularly the sweet woman across the hall, Lisa. Once the neurologist released me from the hospital. Ruby, my friend from the support group, picked me up after a three-week stay, two of them in a coma.

I'm supposed to be in seclusion. Donovan knows. He found me. He always did. They assured me I would be safe, but I'll never be safe if Donovan's alive. Nervous energy kept me from sitting, and I peered outside the dark draperies hanging from the front window of Ruby's small bungalow. His mother texted, asking me to please return home, swearing that she'd keep Donovan in line. How could she do that when she couldn't keep her own husband in check? Donovan's loud sports car drove by often, enough to terrorize me. Peeking through the window, I saw him glaring at the house. Ruby's house was on the edge of town. Although clean, it was a small wooden structure. If you blew hard enough, it might just fall down. I felt no safer here than at home. Donovan saw me watching, and he jerked his hand, four fingers in a fist and his thumb pointing west. I knew that meant to get home. He did it enough times when we were at his parent's house for dinner for me to recognize the meaning. I waited until Ruby left for the grocery store and walked home, miles in the heat, the pain intolerable. He knew because he drove by several times, sneering at me. Not once offering me a ride. Toward the end of his life, it was the constant sexual assaults that did me in. Made my decision. If I couldn't get away, he had to die.

You might wonder how things turned so bad so quickly. I can't answer that. It was as though a light bulb went off in Donovan and he became an abusive monster. Each hospitalization resulted in urine-soaked clothing and a closet filled with the acrid odor upon my return home. How much more can I humanly endure? I'm only twenty-five and I'm ready to die.

〜

THE FULL MOON HANGS HIGH. DONOVAN WILL BE WORSE THAN usual tonight. A full moon makes the crazies come out. Something my grandmother always said. How much eviler can Donovan get? In this marriage, I'm tossed by a force greater than me. His anger and hatred propelled him. I can't breathe or think. I'm dying inside a little more each day. It's dark. It's chaotic. I'm drowning in despair. There is only survival. I must not let him kill me. He stepped through the apartment door, I didn't get a chance to determine his demeanor when in a flash, he became infuriated because dinner wasn't ready. In a mere five minutes, the timer would go off for the rice, and we'd eat. Instead, he punched me, and I fell into the refrigerator handle, cutting my head. It always started with my head. He threw me on the kitchen table, shoved my shorts down, and assaulted me while chanting, "You belong to me. I control you and your life. I decide if you live or die." To drown out his voice, his smell, him, I imagined myself at the beach, anything to escape my life and his hands groping me. The azure water hits the sand. I smelled the salt. Felt the warm sand between my toes. He finished before the timer went off for the rice. After the first time he hit me, we never made love again. Sex was for control and to violate me. He pulled me up by my hair and punched me in the mouth. The pain was excruciating. I tasted the metallic flavor of blood. I married a psychopath; how did I not know this? My two front teeth landed on the floor. At that moment, I wished for death. I whimpered a high squeal, a pathetic sound. I hated myself more than him. How many times had he pulled my hair and dragged me into the bedroom to rape me, my legs scrambling behind to release the pressure on my scalp? Yes, it was rape. I was not a willing participant. I hurried into the bathroom and rinsed my mouth to survey the damage. My two front teeth were gone and the two next to them on both sides were loose. This was finally my 'Ah Ha' moment, the proverbial light bulb illuminated, and

I realized he must die in order for me to live. I was not only in a marriage lacking love, but it was also violent and dangerous.

Donovan kept his pills on the nightstand. I removed four, using my dishwashing gloves, my hands shaking. I hid the pills in my jeans pocket and returned to the kitchen. "Get me whiskey, bitch!" Donovan demanded, sitting like a king at the head of the table. The same table he just used to force himself on me. I reached for the pills, crushed two, and poured the powdery residue inside the glass. I slid the glass in front of him. My hands trembled; dare I? He grabbed it roughly and gulped it down without even noticing the pill residue. I didn't care if he saw it. One of us was going to die tonight, and I hoped it was him. He took a forkful of rice, shoved the chicken into his mouth as though he hadn't eaten in months. He polished off the whiskey. Bile forced its way into my throat, watching the devil sitting across from me. My parents taught me not to hate, raised me to love everyone, even damaged people. I learned in school that the devil was below, in hell. But he wasn't. He walked the earth and was sitting at the kitchen table. Donovan was someone I couldn't love or even remotely like. My hatred for him ran deep. He had to stop, and tonight would be the night. I sat trying to eat and act as normally as possible, trying to distract myself from my burning female part, inflamed by his latest rough attack. Not to mention my missing teeth. I knew I couldn't throw away the small amount of food on my plate, otherwise I'd be disciplined for being wasteful.

After I cleaned the kitchen, his eyes drooped, and he yawned repeatedly, yet demanded another drink and a snack to watch football games he had recorded. Footage of the games he played in at college, usually after watching his performance, he would get aroused. After all wasn't he the big man on campus? He wasn't getting near me ever again, not sexually, not physically. Two more pills went into his second whiskey. The video was short, and he walked past me and into the bedroom. He yelled, "Get in here and suck me off!"

My patience and will to live was gone, and I yelled back, "No, get one of your whores to do it." His arm swung out as I took a backhand to my face for my response, then took his muscle relaxers from the same bottle I took pills from earlier. He added two pain killers and climbed into bed.

Struggling to concentrate, I sat in the bedroom chair with an open book on my lap, my head throbbing with blood clots in my hair. My shoulder felt as though Donovan had dislocated it again. *This is the last time, Donovan, the last time you'll hurt me.* Suddenly, he snorted, and his body convulsed. I jumped up and felt torn. *Should I help? Wake him or just let the medications take care of him?* Painfully rising from the chair, I headed to the bathroom to wash off the blood from my hair and face. Inside the small shower enclosure, I tried to wash the clotted blood from my hair. After cleaning up the aftermath of the sexual assault, I plopped on the shower floor, shaking and sobbing. It was how I lived, always shaking and sobbing. After drying off, I changed into pajamas and slid next to him in bed, so tired of being beaten and violated and drained from being in pain. I smelled the vomit before I saw it on his chest and tried to wake him; he didn't move, and I dialed 9-1-1.

"9-1-1, what's your emergency?" The female voice came through clearly on the line.

"My husband, I don't think he's breathing!" I gasped.

"Okay, stay on the line. I have medics and police responding."

"Okay." I sob. *What have I done?*

"Is he moving?" The operator asked me.

"No, I can't get him to wake up!" I sobbed. *I've done it, I'm afraid.* Tears flowed down my face and onto my nightgown. *I'm frightened. Will God forgive me for taking his life, ending my pain, the torture?* My head bled again, mingling with my short, dark hair. I reached for a towel and pressed it to the wound. I'd cut my hair short to give Donovan less to pull. Pounding on the door startled me, and I scurried to the front of the apartment and pulled the door open. A familiar face greeted me. This young officer has been to the house many times because the neighbors called during Donovan's reign of terror. I pointed to the bedroom as the medics hurried inside to Donovan.

They returned with Donovan on a stretcher. Heat rose to my face, blood pulsed in my ears as black spots appeared in front of my eyes. Voices in the apartment sounded distant, almost as though they were under water. I woke in an ambulance, disoriented and sick to my stomach. The medic passed me an emesis basin, and I emptied the contents of my stomach, which wasn't much because I barely ate in Donovan's presence. I'm so thin my clothing hung on me, but Donovan hadn't cared. He ridiculed the amount of food on my plate. He didn't want a fat wife.

They declared Donovan dead before I could reach the emergency room. Hospitalization was necessary, and the medical staff provided me with fluids and antibiotics. I cried, not because he was gone, but because I was going to hell for murdering him. Tears of relief replaced the tears of guilt. As I wiped my tears, the young officer who's been at our house often stepped in to question me. I gazed into his kind eyes when he began, "Mrs. King, I'm sorry for your pain. I need to ask you a few questions. Are you feeling up to it? Do you remember me? I'm Jacob Swanson."

I quickly covered my mouth so he wouldn't see the gaping hole. "Yes, officer." The tears flowed again, butterflies swarmed my stomach, and I felt my heart beating as though it was visible through the thin material of the hospital gown. My hands trembled.

"You can call me Jacob." He inhaled and asked, "Did your

husband abuse prescription drugs?" I nodded. "Why did he take them?"

"For football injury, in college, three years ago. Ruined what Donovan hoped would be a career in pro football."

"Do you know what he took?"

"Percocet and muscle relaxers. He seemed to have an endless supply of them. The muscle relaxers he got from his doctor."

"Did the percs make him mean?"

"Kinda," I lied, "But he had a mean streak before them, they just made it worse. Added, Donovan hated his job because he felt he should have held a management position and not start at the bottom." I took a deep breath. "He also thought he should have been playing pro football."

"You know, I responded to many of the domestic calls that came in about you two. Yet the calls never came from you, always neighbors."

"He would have killed me if I called." I wiped my tears with the tissue he offered me from the nightstand.

"Why did you rescind the restraining orders?"

"I didn't. But he'd ignore them and still find me, and when he did, it wasn't pretty. I couldn't seem to hide from him. The system couldn't keep me safe."

"I'm so sorry we failed you. I'm hoping to make it better for others."

"It's not possible. The police cannot manage it since they are already stretched too thin. Not to mention other factors come into play."

"Such as?"

"Payoffs. Not the police, but Donovan's family has a lot of money and prestige. They had several restraining orders squashed. My father-in-law plays golf with the judge. It became pointless." I shrugged.

Donovan's parents made the funeral arrangements, despite me telling them I should. Well, I guess not on the grand scale they could do it, anyway. It was an entire day's affair, starting with the viewing at their church. Row after row of people crowded in to mourn the monster's death. I sat between his father and his mother. I sobbed dutifully. Not because I grieved. I was petrified because I did this to their son.

His mother held my hand as she gently dabbed her eyes with a fancy handkerchief. I sat with silent tears pouring from my face, wishing for my parents. My brothers. Never have I ever felt so alone. The guilt was tearing me up inside.

The funeral celebration felt like it lasted an eternity. The choir sang beautiful hymns, and the congregation stood, singing and clapping as though it were a normal Sunday. Not like any of the somber funerals I attended back in New York.

Donovan's brass casket shined brightly in the sunlight that streamed through the stained-glass windows. They placed his college graduation photo on the closed lid. It was the only thing I asked for. The closed casket. His parents reluctantly agreed. I couldn't imagine standing there, seeing his face. Closed I could get through it.

After the never-ending service, they escorted us to the cemetery. I rode in the limousine with my in-laws. A handkerchief over my mouth so no one would see the damage. Worried, I turned toward the window and gazed outside, not to meet their eyes. They were already upset enough learning he abused drugs. He did, but I only added to them as he often did.

The sun was bright as we exited the vehicle. Shoving my sunglasses on my nose, I cast my gaze to the trees. The gentle sway of the leaves calmed me. My father-in-law placed his palm on the small of my back and the other on his wife's. The funeral director placed Donovan's casket onto a stand over the vacant space that opened for his last resting place. Flowers from the church surrounded it. The funeral director placed the photo on top of the casket, and Donovan's smiling face seemed to follow me. I remember that day vividly; he was in a great mood. After taking our photos, Donovan treated me to lunch. We laughed, teased, and shared each other's food. That was the Donovan I loved.

Before I knew it, the minister asked the guests to place a flower on the casket. After doing so, everyone went to their cars. My father-in-law went next. He said a prayer, kissed his fingers and placed them on his son's photo. His mother was worse. Heartbreaking. She tried to lie across the casket when her husband pulled her back. She reached for the photo and brought it to her chest. I watched as they walked away. I stayed. Staring at the casket, the tears pouring down my cheeks, landing on my black blouse, I whispered, "Goodbye, Donovan." I turned away and walked toward a better tomorrow. It sounds harsh, but what else could I say to the man who beat me, put me in comas, left scars on my body? Destroyed me. Knocked my teeth out. My father-in-law waited, squeezed my shoulder as I entered the limo to the funeral luncheon.

The in-laws hosted the meal at their house rather than the country club. There were so many friends of my in-laws and Donovan's, offering condolences, striking up conversations. Noise in my head. I wouldn't ever remember any of them. I overheard so many people whispering, "She's so young to be a widow," or "Do you think she messed with drugs, too? After all, she is from the big city and probably introduced him to the high." Brandie and I mostly stayed in the kitchen with the catering staff to escape the whispers. It wasn't until late that evening I could get back to the apartment. Brandie never strayed far from my side. She took me home, asked me to pack a bag. She wanted to take me to her apartment. Refusing at first, but upon smelling the familiar stale odor of the building, I nodded in agreement. It was Brandie who steadfastly stayed by my side and eventually helped me move. I was heartbroken when she moved to California for a job, as I'd grown fond of the sweet girl.

Several months after the funeral, Donovan's mother knocked on the door. She came bearing gifts. A candle and a bouquet. Over coffee, she mentioned she had some money that her husband didn't know about, and she wanted to get my mouth fixed. After refusing her kind offer several times, I finally agreed.

After seeing the dentist, I sported a brand-new smile with dental implants. She sat with me at every appointment. When the doctor asked how it happened, I lied about the car accident. I couldn't embarrass her by saying her son did it. The man I referred to in my mind as the devil's spawn. My confidence was slowly coming back, although I still panicked when I heard a raised voice. I survived the worst of the storms, or so I thought until now. I had no one to shield me from the devil himself because I told no one.

I lost touch with my in-laws. My mother-in-law took Donovan's death hard; he was her only child. My father-in-law suffered as well and retired from his job to care for his wife. She wasn't functioning any longer and rarely left the house. Thorton thought it best for me to stay away. My presence in their lives was too much for her because I reminded her of what she lost, her son and potential grandchildren. This was the least I could do for her since I was thankful for her when she got my mouth fixed and understood this was best for all of us. I needed a fresh start as well, and the only connection to them was Donovan, and he was dead. So, I guess to them I needed to be too. It was okay. I was thankful for the help, the dental work, the clothing. Sometimes I'd find cash in my purse. I knew it was Shirley slipping me the money. She was the best part of my marriage.

Three

onths later, I applied for a job as a counselor in a women's crisis center in the city. The same center who workers referred attendees to the support group. While working there, I met my best friend, Savannah. She escaped her abusive husband in California and moved home to Texas, to our town far from where she grew up. She told her horror stories and offered her apartment to anyone needing to get away. Donovan's life insurance money was used to secure a small cottage as a deposit while I saved the rest. I also adopted a kitten from the shelter. I enjoyed my new life, although my parents were upset that I hadn't moved back to New York after the funeral. Although Texas was far, I loved my friends from the support group and the area. Being surrounded by traffic in the city wasn't something I missed. I lived in that cottage for two years, spent many nights with abuse victims in the hospital as our group had done for me. I took pets into my home until the victims could get on their feet. We were a family, a family of wounded misfits.

While helping Ruby with orchestrating the meetings, I never shared my story. Ruby felt it would be helpful to the other ladies. One woman was a sweet older woman who wore sneakers with Velcro closures, claiming they were the best shoes ever invented. Reading glasses dangled around her neck with a multitude of different chains. Some chains on her reading glasses were beaded, while others were not. She tried to match her outfit with the neckwear for the day. All bought from the Dollar store. Her shoes rarely changed, always white, always with Velcro closures. Her blouses were mostly floral patterned. For casual attire, she wore elastic waisted jeans and alternated between light and dark denim. Neatly pressed with seams down the legs, so sharp they appeared professionally pressed by the dry cleaner in town. Ruby found ironing therapeutic. She wore her hair the same way every day in a cute pixie cut. Like many others, she sheared off her hair, so her abuser couldn't use it as leverage. It was less expensive to get her hair cut at the barbershop. Vanity had long since gone out the window as she aged.

It still took months for me to gather my courage. Ruby felt my stories would offer hope to the women that there was a life to be had. A good one.

The night she scheduled me to speak was warm. The night sky was littered with bright stars. Yet the brightness didn't reach my heart. Fear gripped me. Scared of reliving it, of opening old wounds, and perhaps my confession would spill from my lips. I planned on sharing one incident. Some were worse than others, even though they were all horrid. This was a harrowing story; I still tremble when I think about it. I know it by heart and don't need to write it down.

After leaving the office, I headed home to change into something comfortable. I wore my favorite jeans and a soft green T-shirt, and I slid into my favorite sneakers. I microwaved leftover pasta, fed the cat, and ate a small bowl of pasta. Before heading to church, I gave myself a pep talk. *You can do this. Everyone knows not to share stories outside of the group.*

I stopped at the bakery and ordered my usual two dozen. Jimmy always emptied the case and gave us more. He usually locked up and headed home after waiting for me. He's a lovely older man who recently lost his wife. Small and thick in the waist, a strip of white surrounded the bald spot in the center of his head.

Upon arrival, I found Ruby waiting for me in the parking lot. Ruby climbed the church steps as I arrived. She took one box from me, and we headed to the old Bible study classroom and set up. I dropped a box off in the room across the hall that hosted the AA meeting. Pastor Robinson already had the coffee going. I stepped over and placed the confections on the table. "Good evening, Pastor," I tapped the white pastry box. "There's a bear claw in this one. I know it's your favorite."

"Oh dear, I probably shouldn't." He mentioned as he pulled the lid open. "It's a beautiful one! Perfectly shaped and glazed." His reach was tentative, almost as though he thought I would tap his hand like a person would to a child.

"Jimmy said it was especially for you."

"He's a good man, that Jimmy, his Doris too. God rest her soul." I smile, having only met Doris twice. She was a sweet woman. She called everyone, "Sugar." When we met, she commented on my eye color and said, "Sugar, those eyes are like stunning glass candy, a lot of sugar and a little spicy, like a mojito with extra lime. I bet you can only be sweet. Those are the prettiest green eyes I ever saw." The memory made me smile.

The ladies began arriving one by one, along with the only gentleman, Parker. He's sweet. Around my age, he told us his stepfather abused and allegedly killed his mother. He offered support, security, and he refilled the coffee. Parker often brought chocolates for the ladies. He's our self-appointed security.

At seven, Parker stuck his head into the hallway to make sure it was clear, and he closed the door. I stepped to the podium and smiled. "Welcome everyone. Does anyone want to share how your week went?"

A few ladies murmur, "Okay," or "He's away on business," more of the same. I realized Ruby must have mentioned I was going to speak, and they were eager to hear my story. I sipped my coffee, gazed around the room, and saw Pastor Robinson sitting in the last row with Parker.

"Many of you know my name. For those that don't, it's Andressa. My husband abused me for several years until he overdosed. I was only twenty-two years old when we eloped and moved from Florida to his hometown in Texas. His abuse began with a pinch here and there. Then it escalated to shoving, maybe a slap or two. As his personality changed, he became meaner. This story is hard to tell, but I will share it. It was a warm Saturday; I went to the grocery store to do my weekly shopping. I thought it odd that he didn't call like usual. My fully charged phone wouldn't respond. Hurrying through the store, I finished and paid for the food." I inhaled.

"When I returned home, he paced outside of our building. I pulled into our assigned spot, and he hurried over and climbed into the backseat. He asked if I bought him cigarettes. A new habit he developed. I mentioned there was a carton in the desk drawer. He insisted there weren't any. I spent my allotment on food already. He insisted he gave me extra money for cigarettes." I sipped my coffee. He hadn't." After a deep breath, I continued. "His eyes looked off, and he seemed fidgety. He insisted I pull out of the spot and head toward the highway. I mentioned I had to go to the bathroom. Could he wait while I ran inside? He refused and pulled my hair, grabbing it with his fist it so I couldn't get out of the car. I followed his directions, and we ended up on Main Street outside a bar. He told me he had to meet someone. We waited while my bladder felt like it would explode. When the man called Mack didn't show, I told him I would go inside and find him. He forbade it. I was about to wet myself when I jumped from the car and ran inside the bar. I used the restroom and asked for Mack. A beefy man stood and followed me outside. Donovan was outside the car, his face was blood red, wearing a grimace. He pounded his fist into the car, denting it. I slipped past him and climbed into the driver's seat while he conversed with Mack. Donovan climbed back into the back seat and slid to the middle, straddling the hump on the floor. He muttered, "We gotta wait. He doesn't have what I need."

"Stupidly, I argued that the food in the trunk would go bad. I put the car in gear to go home when he put a pocketknife to my throat." I wiped my tears and sipped from the water bottle Ruby handed me and continued. "We were still in the parking lot six hours later, with a dead phone because he hadn't paid the bill and a trunk full of meats, the ice cream he wanted and frozen food. In the summer heat in Texas. He kept the knife trained at my throat the entire time. We waited until Mack came out of the bar and stepped to the driver's window and asked if I was okay. It was dark and Donovan pushed the knife point to my neck. I told him I was okay, and I knew if I said something about the knife, Donovan would make things much worse. Explaining that Donovan wanted to wait. Mack looked at Donovan with hatred in his eyes. He tossed a small baggie in the car, hitting Donovan in the face. After Mack left, Donovan kept the knife at my throat until we got home." I touched the small C shaped keloid on my neck. "He cut me when the car hit a bump in the road. This scar is from that evening. He was so high when we got home, he crashed on the sofa. I was grateful because I didn't get beaten that night." As I stepped away from the podium, I heard sympathetic murmurs. Ruby took over while I freshened up in the ladies' room.

Pastor Robinson waited behind to help. Usually, Parker locked the church since our pastor went to his rooms early. "Andressa, that was a horrible story. You are a strong woman. God is watching over you, my dear. I'll pray for your continued healing. Goodnight and God Bless you." He squeezed my shoulder and left. He blessed me, and I appreciated it more than anyone could understand, having been raised in a Godly home.

Our weekly meeting provided socialization not only for me, but for the ladies. I made a few friends who were dealing with abuse, too. I'm grateful I can help them. Even if it's just a place to socialize and get things off their chest.

One week led to another, the faces in the meetings changed from week to week. Some were too bruised and embarrassed to show up, others were in the hospital with another standing guard. Ruby and I worked as a team. We split our evenings on guard in the hospital.

My friendship with Savannah flourished. We drove to work together, each of us taking turns. I had traded in Donovan's sports car for a newer sedan. My first car.

The craziest thing was that Savannah and I looked so much alike. Except for the eyes. Mine were green, and hers were a warm coffee color. We were the same height and almost weighed the same. We bonded over books and music. She was a quick reader while I was much slower because I suffered from migraines. We were a two-woman book club. We started hanging out after work, too.

As the only single women at work, we spent a lot of time together. At the office they called us "The Doppelgangers." Movies, dinners, concerts and shopping excursions were our favorite things to do. Savannah had a wonderful sense of humor. She had everyone in stitches with her witty and sarcastic humor.

We did everything together; it was like living as teenagers all over again. We went to concerts in the park, dancing, movie nights, sleepovers.

The first trip we took together was to visit her older brother in Columbia. Boy, was he intense but handsome. Shoulder length, almost black hair and dark brown eyes. His eyes were penetrating unless he gazed at his sister, then they softened. He rarely left the compound, tending to his business by the ocean. Although busy, he ensured they brought us into town for fancy dinners or shopping excursions.

Savannah and I spent most of our days on the beach. Alejandro had food delivered to us, along with fruity drinks. The day before our flight home, he joined us on the beach. His interactions with his much younger sister were always tender. We enjoyed a game of volleyball, us against him. We lost. After cleaning up, Alejandro had the chef prepare a five-course meal in our honor. For a man so cold, he warmed up with those closest to him, and I got to see the real man.

The meal began with sushi, salad, and appetizers, followed by seafood bisque, tender beef, and an olive oil cake with blood orange. I'd never tried the cake before, but it was amazing.

The following morning, as we were waiting for Alejandro's driver, he pulled me aside and thanked me for loving his sister and being her best friend. He enveloped me in a warm hug.

While waiting for our flight, Savannah turned to me and said, "Ugh, he is so intense sometimes. If he knew what Bart put me through, he'd hunt him down. It wouldn't be pretty."

"He is intense, but Sav when he looks at you, his face changes. He loves you so much."

"I love him too. He was ten when I was born. He was more of a father to me than mine."

"Really?"

"Yeah, our Papa was always busy. A workaholic. I think Alejandro gets it from him. I wish he would marry. He'd be an amazing papa." The flight was called. We stepped onto the plane and Savannah promptly fell asleep. I peeked into our bag of candy and realized my friend and her sweet tooth had polished off the gummy bears. I settled for a piece of a chocolate bar and popped my ear buds in to listen to a podcast.

Four

Two years after Donovan's death, my hair had grown in and was longer and healthy. These days, I have a few extra pounds on me and I'm smiling more often. Even though my work was sad, I still felt happy. I made a positive difference; I fought every day for the women's safety.

I also learned that my former mother-in-law, Shirley, passed away in her sleep. After reaching out to Thorton with condolences, he asked me not to attend the services. I agreed it was time to move on and thanked him for taking my call. I later learned he married his administrative assistant and was expecting a little girl. Hopefully, he's treating his new wife better than he did Shirley.

I was craving my mother's Feijao Tropeiro, a traditional dish made with beans, bacon, sausage, collard greens, eggs and manioc flour so I hurried to the grocery store after work. My mother, not of Brazilian descent, loved most of the food and often prepared them for my father. I'd looked through the collard greens when a cart banged into mine as I loaded up my grocery cart with fresh vegetables,

"I'm so sorry, ma'am, I should have been paying better attention."

"No problem," I said, when I looked up and saw a familiar face, yet one I couldn't place.

"Mrs. King?"

"I was. It's Oliveira now. I went back to my original name. You're familiar to me. I know we've met, yet I cannot remember where."

"Jacob Swanson, Officer Jacob Swanson."

Heat invaded my face, and I knew it was pink. "I remember now. My apologies, you look different out of uniform." I stammered. He was dressed in jeans and a blue plaid shirt that made his azure eyes even bluer than I remembered. My stomach knotted up. If anyone were suspicious that I fed the pills to Donovan, it would be him as the first responder.

"No need to apologize, Ma'am."

"Oh, please call me Andressa."

"Andressa, you look well." He stammered, his cheeks bright, almost as though he thought he was offensive. "Would you like to get a coffee with me?" He thumbed toward the little café in the grocery store's front. "There's a coffee shop right there." He pointed again, noticing my hesitation.

I'd already grabbed a cup when I walked in, but I hadn't let him know, "Sure, I'd love to." *Be careful, Andressa, this could be a trap!* I don't know why that thought flooded my consciousness.

Over coffee, we got to know each other, and he asked me to go to dinner the next night. He was off duty for the weekend and didn't have plans. Outside of work and the support group, I rarely socialized. I liked Jacob, even when he called me Andi a few times. No one had called me Andi, and I loved hearing him say it with his slight drawl.

After two weeks of dating, Jacob invited me to a concert in the park. He brought a blanket and a picnic basket. It was the most romantic date I'd ever experienced. He was always the gentleman, and most nights kissed my cheek good night. During the concert, he held my hand, poured the wine, and toasted to us. I was falling in love, and it scared me. He was so much like my father, gentle, kind, and funny.

After the concert, Jacob held my hand as we walked to the car. He made me feel special, and he listened to me, really listened. We shared work stories and childhood stories. He was sweet and treated me kindly, and it wasn't hard to like him. Falling in love with him came easily. I missed him when he worked. I lived for his calls each day. He always started with, "Hello beautiful." He seemed to know when I needed a call the most. My cat, who liked only me, liked him too. If he sat on the sofa, she'd cuddle in his lap. I knew animals were the true test of a good person. Jacob was a good person.

We took things slowly. Sex hadn't come up in the conversation, nor did he try anything inappropriate. We'd kissed, and I hadn't met a sweeter gentleman. He was also a member of the small local church I'd joined, the same church that hosted our support group. We dated for three months when Jacob planned a vacation. He wanted to see New York City. One of his college friends had moved to the city to pursue a career on Broadway, and he'd invited me along. Savannah offered to watch my cat. Callie liked her.

We flew to New York in May and planned to be there for the long Memorial Day weekend. Since my parents had downsized and currently lived in an apartment, we booked adjoining rooms in a hotel in Manhattan. Jacob had made reservations at Carmine's for the two of us on our first night. I bought a new dress for dinner; I'd only been there one time before for a friend's birthday and was excited to enjoy the experience as an adult.

The restaurant staff seated us at a romantic table for two upon our arrival. It was during dessert that Jacob stepped over to me and bent on one knee. "Andressa, a beautiful name for a beautiful woman. I love you; I think I fell in love with you when you were that short-haired waif that I stood guard over. Will you marry me?" The tears poured down my face, a full-blown ugly girl cry. "Andi?" Jacob raised his eyebrows.

"Yes, I would love to marry you. I love you too!" I replied. He placed a beautiful diamond ring on my finger, and I couldn't stop looking at it and him.

He sat back down, grinning. "I don't need a long engagement, honey; I just want to marry you." He leaned back on the chair, smiling.

"I don't need one either. You say the word, and I'll be there," I replied, smiling back at him.

"I don't have a big family. Just my mom and me. But I want a nice honeymoon, to spend it with you, the love of my life."

"I'd love a honeymoon! Maybe a cruise? Have you ever been on a cruise, Jacob?"

"No, and I think that would be awesome!" He said, taking a spoonful of tiramisu.

"Me too! I'd always dreamed of a cruise honeymoon. Oh, Jacob, I'm so happy!"

"Me too, beautiful, me too!" his blue eyes smiled back at me.

We visited my parents after dinner. Where I'd learned that Jacob had swiped my phone and copied my parent's phone number, my sweet man called and asked for my hand in marriage. As if I didn't love him enough already.

That night we'd made love for the first time. I remember it so vividly; it was romantic. We went back to the hotel; Jacob went into his room and a few minutes later, he knocked on the adjoining door. I had just slipped out of my heels and was just about to undress for bed. I walked over and unlocked the door. Jacob waited, grinning with champagne. He took off his tie and rolled up his shirt sleeve. Butterflies surged in my stomach; he was so handsome. "We should toast our engagement and plan the honeymoon." He motioned to his tablet under his left arm.

We sat next to each other on the bed and drank champagne. Jacob found a cruise that left Texas and we planned to be married the day before. We decided on a small ceremony at church and would stream it live for my sick grandparents to watch. My brothers agreed to fly out and walk me down the aisle, stepping in for my father, who felt torn because his parents were so ill and me getting married. I assured my dad that it was fine and to stay in New York, where his parents needed him. Jacob booked the cruise from our hotel room and paid for it in full on his credit card.

I turned to him and said, "I'm excited to be your wife." He turned and kissed me deeply and passionately, the most passionate kiss that I ever experienced. He eased open my mouth with his tongue, and I felt the heat course through my body. I felt as though my heart thrummed deep into my womanhood. Jacob pulled me from the bed and helped me out of my dress. He pulled me back into his arms, and I felt his desire against me. I unbuttoned his shirt and pulled it off of him. My hand touched his muscular chest and then slid down towards his belt buckle. I froze and became uncertain. He slipped my hand aside and unbuckled his belt. Then he unfastened his slacks, which eventually dropped to the floor. He stood in his boxer briefs, his erection pushing forward. He slid my bra down, one strap at a time, paying equal attention to my breasts. I experienced feelings I hadn't felt before. He reached his hand into my panties and found that special collection of nerve endings. The heat between my legs intensified, and I squeezed Jacob's shoulder. He guided me back to the bed and laid half on top of me. He slid my panties down and off. Jacob removed his briefs and kissed me again. He entered me slowly at first and then plunged inside of me. I experienced my first orgasm that night as I felt Jacob's pulse through me. He stayed inside of me, and he kissed me. His kisses were terrific, and I could feel his love in his touch.

Afterward, I realized he didn't use protection. I'd gone off the pill after Donovan died, as I didn't plan to marry again or be intimate with anyone. I laid my head on Jacob's chest and said, "I guess I should have mentioned this before, but I'm not on the pill or anything."

"No way?" He teased. "Me either. I forgot to refill them!" He joked and kissed my head. "Honey, if it happens, it happens. I'm ready to be a dad. Are you ready to be a mom?"

"I think I am ready. Jacob, that was so romantic, and I experienced my first..." Tears glistened in my eyes as heat flooded my cheeks.

"Oh, honey, I'm happy that you had it with me." He pulled me closer and held me tight, kissing the top of my head.

Our trip to New York was a whirlwind. I met his friend, Teddy, who would fly to Texas to attend our wedding. I asked Savannah to be my matron of honor and Jacob asked Parker to be his best man.

On our flight home, Jacob asked Callie and me to move in with him. His house was a beautiful two-story, with a huge backyard and an in-ground pool. He bought it from the bank and had done a lot of work to update it. I'd been there before, and while it was still under remodeling, it was a lovely home in a great school district. I agreed and put my small cottage up for sale.

Our wedding day quickly approached, in the later part of summer. I wished I could have waited for the fall foliage to hit the area, but it typically happens by November when you'd see shades of orange, red and yellow across the state. Neither Jacob nor I wanted to wait that long. Our wedding day dawned with the glorious, cloudless sky. The bright sun glistened off the pool water. Jacob left early to get ready at Parker's house, leaving me and my brothers to get ready in our home. The dress I chose was knee-length cream lace with short cap sleeves and a modest scoop neckline. I wore a string of pearls around my neck, a gift from Glory, my new mother-in-law. Her late husband presented them on her wedding day. My hair was long and curled, with a white pearled comb holding up one side. Longer on the other side to cover the scar. I didn't want memories of Donovan on my special day.

My brothers drove me to the church in their rental car. I wasn't nervous, but joyful, knowing I would marry the man that made my heart sing. The ceremony was brief, spiritual, and meaningful. My brothers set up a live feed for my parents and grandparents to watch. We enjoyed a small brunch at our favorite restaurant later. That evening, we drove to Galveston and checked into a hotel for the night. We made love through the night and took the hotel shuttle to the port to board our ship. I was so excited I couldn't stop taking pictures with my cell phone. Jacob was so loving and patient with me. I still had a long way to go to heal emotionally, but Jacob sensed when I needed the support the most. He'd whisper, "You are fine, love; everything is okay."

The honeymoon was nothing short of incredible. During the cruise, we made love often, went on tours, and enjoyed almost everything the ship offered. I loved the days we spent in Mexico. The crystal blue waters were breathtaking. We went to the beach, frolicked in the water like teenagers. I even wore a bikini despite my scars. When we made love, Jacob often kissed each scar, whispering sweet words. One day, while we sat on the beach, a vendor came by with a trained monkey. I hurried over to meet the little animal. Jacob paid to have my picture taken with it. My favorite shot was her sitting on my head. After seven glorious days filled with love and romance, we disembarked, tanned and happy to be starting our new life, yet sad that our honeymoon was over. We returned to our home, where Callie waited. My brothers stayed behind and took care of the house and the cat for us. They enjoyed having the pool in the backyard and asked if they could visit again soon.

Our marriage was terrific from the first day. We made love often, rarely disagreed, and thoroughly enjoyed each other's company. I now knew what it felt like to have a best friend in a husband. I could make mistakes, be late with a meal, burn a shirt while ironing it, and never fear his anger or violence. The only sadness that intruded on us were the migraines I suffered from, several a week. I pushed through them to enjoy my life and my job. Jacob noticed my facial expressions when I was in pain. He would comfort me by tucking me into bed, dimming the lights, and placing cold towels on my head. I hadn't suffered from migraines before Donovan, and the doctors said it was from the years of taking hits, kicks and punches to the head.

I went to work each day and still attended the support group, mostly because these people were family to me. If Jacob weren't on duty, he would come with me, quietly setting up donuts, cookies, and coffee he'd provide. If he were working and not on a call, he'd drop by with snacks. The roughest shifts were four to twelve. He'd be gone before I got off work, and I'd try most nights to stay up and wait for him.

On Valentine's Day, I learned I was pregnant. I suspected it for a few days since I was late but wanted to find out on the most romantic day of the year. Thankfully, Jacob was on the first shift, and we had a romantic dinner planned for the evening. Before leaving work, I took the test I bought at lunchtime, and it was positive. I stowed the stick away in my purse, and my plan was to inform Jacob at dinner. All day long, I pondered on the most romantic way to let him know. I stopped at the greeting card store and got him a card that said, *Happy*

Valentine's Day Daddy. I bought a small gift box for the test and had it wrapped at the store.

After we'd placed our order with the server, Jacob passed me a wrapped box. Inside, I found a diamond-encrusted heart pendant. "Cheesy, I know, sweetie, but you stole my heart, and when I saw this on the television, I had to get it for you," Jacob said, grinning.

"Oh, Jacob, I love it. And it's not cheesy. It's utterly romantic!" I said as I passed him his gift. I never received gifts from Donovan. Just his fists.

He opened the card from me first and then the engraved watch. "Wow, Love, it's awesome! The crazy thing is I dropped my watch this morning, and it shattered."

"I'm happy that I got you something you like and needed," I said as I passed him the other card and the small box.

"Another gift? Honey, the watch is more than enough!"

"Open it, please." I could barely hold back my excitement.

Jacob opened the card first. His brows furrowed in confusion. When he opened the box and saw the plus sign. He stared at me, his mouth open and his eyes wide. "For real? You're pregnant?"

"We're pregnant!"

Jacob jumped out of his chair so quickly. He knocked it over. He pulled me out of my seat and pressed his body to mine, his arms wrapped around me. Every day, every minute, I felt his love. I hoped he felt mine, too. God blessed me with this amazing man.

Further into the pregnancy, I took a few vacation days and cleaned out the bedroom we planned to use for our baby girl. Most of the boxes were mine. I found the journals I kept hidden from Donovan, where I wrote of every horror. I wanted to move on and leave him in my past, despite the guilt I suffered through. My mother knew how I loved to write in a journal and would send me a cute notebook or an actual journal often. Later that evening, Jacob asked me if I had any trash from the cleanup. I mentioned a box that I kicked at the top of the stairs. He thought the journals were a mistake and left them on the kitchen table before heading out for the second shift.

I opened one book, the one I bought before we left Florida. I thought I should start a new book to begin a new life. Palm trees and the beach adorned the cover.

MAY 1

WE DID IT! DONOVAN AND I GOT MARRIED. I CAN'T WAIT TO BEGIN our lives together. He took me to a romantic dinner after and then to a hotel on the water. It wasn't one of the nicest places, but it was clean and romantic. It kind of felt different being married. He was happy; I love my wedding ring. It's white gold with circle etchings. His ring is just a plain white gold band. It was what he wanted.

MAY 15

YAY! THE DAY IS FINALLY HERE! GRADUATION. IT WAS HARD STAYING in the dorms without my hubs. He struggled a lot more than I did. Today, we grabbed our diplomas and we hit the road. There wasn't any point in me "walking" since my grandparents were ill, and my parents couldn't come. I understood. Donovan hated all the rehearsals and when he learned I wasn't planning on walking, he agreed we should hit the road early. His dad was furious.

Our trip took longer than eighteen hours, because Donovan wanted to make it a honeymoon. We stopped at a motel the first night. He wanted sex a lot! I was so tired, and he didn't understand why I didn't have an orgasm. I don't know why, but I haven't yet.

. . .

MAY 18

WE GOT THE KEYS TO THE APARTMENT DONOVAN RENTED ONLINE. Huge mistake, it's nasty. Old, smelly, with threadbare carpets. I reassured Donovan, I could make it colorful and nice.

MAY 25

WE SPENT THE WEEK WITH DONOVAN, TRYING TO BRING ME TO orgasm. He's stressing me out and I'm so tender down there. He wants me to go to the doctors. After attending a barbecue at his folk's house, I'm excited for him to start his new job. Our savings accounts are getting low. We combined our accounts and used some of the money for our security deposit and first rent. We went to Dollar General for food. He wouldn't ask his parents for help because he already pissed off his dad that he married me right out of college.

MAY 26

DONOVAN STARTED HIS NEW JOB. HE CALLED ME ON HIS BREAK, UPSET because his father insisted, he begin at the lowest level. The mailroom! He ranted about having a degree and being reduced to sorting mail in the mailroom. The salary was minimum wage. I calmed him down; told him I loved him and would make a special dinner. Donovan loved to eat, and his favorite was carbs, especially spaghetti. We had a jar of sauce and a box of spaghetti, with just the two of us, we could eat it for a few days. When I heard his loud old sports car pull into the parking lot, I waited at the door with a smile and a hug. He seemed grateful. He ate with enthusiasm but was quiet. Afterward, he plopped on the old recliner that was here when we moved in and promptly fell asleep.

   May 28

NOTHING MUCH TO WRITE, MORE OF THE SAME. DONOVAN complained about the monotonous work and his frustration with his father. I kept the house clean and did the laundry, even though I was bored. We were one floor above the community laundry room, which was a huge convenience. On pay day, Donovan came home with a case of beer and a bottle of whiskey. I wasn't worried about it because he usually had just two beers when we were in college.

JUNE 3

DONOVAN IS GETTING OUT OF CONTROL. HE'S DRINKING A LOT. SAYS it helps with the pain from his injury. I made a doctor's appointment for him, and he took the day off and went. The doctor prescribed Percocet and Flexeril. He seems less painful, but his behavior is erratic. He called me fat stuff today. Told me to put less food on my plate since I'm home all day long. I cried, and he made fun of me. I don't have a roll of fat anywhere! While I can't run track, I exercise every day in the house. Aerobics and an abs of steel DVD we found in the apartment. He's tired and I make sure when he comes home from work each day, he gets to relax.

· · ·

I took a break knowing the ugly was coming in the next dozen pages. I shoved the journals into a brown paper bag and into the hall closet. Was it safe to read this kind of stuff while pregnant? I didn't know. Yet they called me. Every time I saw a scar or felt the pain of a long-broken bone, I had this urge to read more. As though remembering would make me see strength or somehow ease the guilt.

Five

J acob took me to lunch at a lovely café next to the paint
store. We chose a light beige for the nursery walls. We'll
go shopping for a crib soon. Being with him is so easy.
He's gentle, he's kind. I like that he places his hand on
the small of my back. I learned not to jump when a touch comes
unexpectedly. The café was old but adorable, something you
would find in a small town. The server was one of our support
group members; she gave me a quick hug on her way to the
kitchen. Although my parents had doubts, I'm happy I stayed in
Texas. This is the good part, my husband, my friends. This was
my first time in this small cafe. The tables were white Formica,
chipped in some spots. The red vinyl booths were lumpy and
repaired with duct tape. It was the smells; the aroma coming
from the kitchen that had me salivating. I groaned. "I'm so
hungry. It smells amazing in here."

"It always does. Sometimes on late shift, my partner and I
come in for a late-night snack." He tapped on my menu. "This is
my favorite burger. Do you want to try it?"

"It sounds yummy, but so does the pulled pork."

"Well, we'll get both, and cut them in half. Does that work, Hon?"

God, I loved this man. I reached across the table and grasped his hand. "That sure does."

After our early lunch, we went to the paint store. I chose the paint, and we headed home so Jacob could ready himself for his shift. I went to the grocery store and bought him a bunch of snacks. "Jacob, these are for your locker. Prepackaged snacks you can take in the patrol car."

"Thanks, gorgeous. Do you go back to work tomorrow?"

"No, I took the rest of the week off. Being pregnant, I'm moving slower than normal."

"You can quit now, babe. I've got us."

"I'm not ready, plus I go on maternity leave soon. They hired someone to fill in behind me. She starts on Monday. I'll train her until the maternity leave kicks in." I smiled, knowing I could tell him anything without repercussions. "Mom and I are headed to San Antonio tomorrow. We going to a baby store in the mall to look at baby stuff and make a wish list."

"I kinda wanted to do that with you. Let me see if I can take a vacation day. We'll make a day of it."

"But your mom will be disappointed."

"No, she won't. We'll pick her up on the way."

Jacob was fortunate to get the day off and, like he said, we made a day of it. We had breakfast in a small family restaurant on the way. Then we ate lunch in this lavish mall. Afterward, we took a walk by the river. Jacob explained the river was a widespread system of rivers, creeks, and streams and channels that cover an area of over four thousand square miles. The river flowed through three hundred miles and through several counties all the way to the Gulf of Mexico. He mentioned the rapid waterbed in town flowed here too. The rapids were below a thick nine-foot wall of stone, trees and root systems. Many accidents happened around this sharp curve. Cars were totaled and occupants killed. So far, no one has survived what was aptly known as Devil's Curve.

"Jacob, it's so scary. Is that where the William's boy died, at that curve?"

"It is, seems to take a life every year. We rarely find the bodies."

Saturday morning dawned with a clear blue sky. Jacob would be home soon after the midnight shift. I prepared a frittata with a side of bacon for his breakfast. He came in so quietly I almost didn't hear him. "Oh honey, I thought you'd still be asleep."

"No, the baby was too active. I got up and made you breakfast." After plating our food, we sat in our chairs. "How was your shift?"

He growled. "Full moon." He rubbed his eyes. "People seemed to misbehave during a full moon. We had a domestic, a fight outside of a bar, and a bunch of kids vandalizing an old building." Sighing, he muttered, "I'm beat."

"Well, finish up and you go to bed. I'll be quiet so you can sleep peacefully."

"Honey, you are always quiet." His eyes twinkled with his smile. "Do what you need to do. If you want to go shopping with Savannah, the paycheck hit our account."

"Maybe a movie instead of shopping."

After the kitchen was tidy, and the laundry done, I pulled out the journals since Savannah had cramps and wanted to stay home to rest.

JUNE *4*

HAPPY ONE-MONTH ANNIVERSARY. OR NOT! DONOVAN CAME HOME IN a foul mood. He said the apartment stunk and was dank. I did the best I could with someone else's stuff. Old stuff. Yes, it carried an odor, but the entire building did. We lived in the oldest and most affordable building in the area. He complained about being forced to live here and that it was all my fault. I asked why and he said it was because he married me. His father wanted him to marry someone else. I told him I would look for a job. It seemed to trigger something dark inside of him. Incredibly dark. He backhanded me across my face. My tooth cut my lip and I bled. He told me, "Clean yourself up, fat ass." I slept on the sofa, alone. How did this happen? Did I miss something about my new husband?

June 5

He returned from work today, sneering. I wasn't speaking to him. After he ate his dinner (I didn't eat), he asked me if I had a problem. Instead of saying, Yeah, you! I ignored him. He then said,

"I don't really care that you're not speaking to me, your accent is harsh and annoying! "He began mimicking me. Oh, so now he hates my New York accent. Well, screw him. I don't normally use that word, but it's appropriate right now. What do I do? Call my folks? My brothers? Admit that I was an idiot and married an asshole?

June 6

We got invited to a fancy cocktail party at his parents', but my lips are still swollen. I iced them all day. I found a nice cocktail dress at Good Will. A basic black dress that I dressed up with costume jewelry that Brandie loaned me. She offered to buy me a dress, this trust fund friend of mine. But I refused. I'm going to find a job and make my way. When she dropped it off, she saw my lip. I lied and said I was playing with a neighbor's puppy, and it nipped at me. Her eyes told me she didn't believe my story.

THE COCKTAIL PARTY WAS HORRIBLE. DONOVAN DIDN'T PERMIT ME to eat anything fattening. He only allowed me to eat the petite lettuce wraps.

It was during the party I learned Donovan was cheating on me. I needed to use the bathroom and my mother-in-law told me to use the upstairs bathroom because the powder room was occupied. As I stepped from the bathroom, Donovan stepped out of his old bedroom with a redhead. At first, they didn't see me. She grabbed his junk and said, "I wish we had time for once more. That was so hot! "

They must have heard my gasp because they both turned. I could tell I scared her, but Donovan sneered. She ran down the set of stairs on the left. Donovan came to me and said, "At least she could come." He walked past me arrogantly. I inhaled so I wouldn't cry. When I went downstairs, I saw my father-in-law waiting for me. He knew! He said something like all men have a side piece. It's not a big deal. You are his wife. He walked away as if cheating were normal! What did I get myself into?

JUNE 15

IT'S BEEN A WHILE, A ROUGH AND HORRIBLE FEW WEEKS. TODAY, Donovan shoved me, and I fell outside the three front steps. I landed hard. He told me, "The fatter you are, the harder you fall." I needed the ER. I'm confident I broke my arm. Or should I say he did? Turns out it was broken. It was his mother who took me to the hospital. All I said when we arrived for dinner was that I fell. She looked at it, her eyes soft, and said, "Come on, let's get to the hospi-tal." On the way, I asked her who the girl was. She told me he was his ex-girlfriend. But not to worry, she is engaged and won't intrude on our marriage. Is she a Stepford wife? Where the hell did I land?

After X-rays, I was told my arm was fractured, my mother-in-law told them a partial truth. I fell down the steps. She didn't mention her asshole son pushed me. After telling him I didn't feel well, and I asked if we could leave earlier than usual. I had horrible cramps and just wanted my bed and a heating pad.

JUNE 30

DONOVAN MADE A MISTAKE AT WORK TODAY. HE LOST A CRITICAL piece of mail. His father yelled at him like a two-year-old. Donovan came home furious and found me napping on the sofa. It didn't matter that I had scraped all the nasty grout from our shower wall and replaced it. Then I scrubbed the bathroom from top to bottom. I don't sleep well anymore and am exhausted. I crashed on the sofa. He came home, found me asleep and pulled me up by my hair and dragged me into the kitchen to make his dinner. Thankfully, I had used the slow cooker and made him a bowl of his favorite chili. He ate with gusto and wiped his bowl clean with cornbread. He belched loudly and plopped down in front of the television. I quickly cleaned up. He went into the bathroom and asked what the smell was. I mentioned I replaced the grout. Instead of acting like a normal husband and expressing his thanks, all he said was, "It's about time." Forgetting myself, I slipped and blurted, "You're welcome." He punched me in my stomach and told me never to sass him again. I needed to get away. But where would I go?

. . .

July 4

I made an icebox cake to take to his parents. They hosted another event for the holiday. Silently, I remind myself. Don't speak. Don't offer an opinion. Smile. Act like a good wife, even though you suck. The things Donovan tells me each time we're with his folks.

Dropping the journal, I laid my head back on the sofa. What I allowed to happen to me was too depressing. I put the journal back in the box and shoved it in the hall closet. Out of sight, it still calls to me. I need to get ready for our first dinner party tonight.

At six, I lit the candles on the dining room table. The candles' warm glow made the room look elegant. We were expecting Parker, Rosie, Savannah, Ruby and, of course, my Glory. My mother-in-law, who I began referring to as my Glory. She was truly a blessing in my life.

I stood in the dining room, admiring my table scape. When Jacob walked in, he smiled at me when our eyes met. I saw the love in his eyes. He quickly stepped over to me and pressed his lips to mine. "Hello gorgeous. Damn, I love that dress on you!" It was a simple wrap dress in emerald green. The saleswoman mentioned it was my color and made my eyes pop. Jacob whispered, "I can't wait to take it off of you later."

I swear my heart raced, kind of like when you had your first crush. I was still crushing on my handsome husband.

The dinner party went well, and Jacob thanked me many times for the delicious food and the beautiful table. He appreciated everything I did and demanded nothing. It brought back not fond memories of another dinner party, this one at friends of Donovan's parents. I couldn't help but compare Donovan to Jacob. They were opposites in every sense of the word.

While the moon's glow cast its light across my sleeping husband, I slipped from the bed and to get the one journal that I used to describe that night. The one that would highlight that night. I think it was the night my inner goddess began planning ways to get out of that marriage. I didn't date this entry, but remembered it was summer.

WE ARRIVED ON TIME, AND I WORE A COCKTAIL DRESS DONOVAN'S mother bought me. Donovan, for once, was kind. He didn't ruin it or me. He was almost gleeful. I felt pretty. His mother is kind to me and wants me to look and feel beautiful. She bought me a pair of silver sandals with low heels. They were so comfortable. The guests were of different ages. The younger crowd hung around the family room while the older adults gravitated to the living room. Dinner was buffet style; an enormous table of delicious foods holding beautiful platters of tempting delights. I put a little on my plate until one of the other wives pulled me along for seconds. We were giggling as we tasted some foods she hadn't tried on the first trip. My first round was a marinated chicken strip on a stick and a few olives. I didn't want to trigger Donovan. Since he was standing by the bar with this woman's husband, I felt braver to try some of the other things, like colossal shrimp cocktail, stuffed bite sized potatoes. I didn't sample any of the dinner type items but enjoyed the appetizers. I glanced up as we shoved potatoes into our mouths, sighing at the creamy taste. My skin tingled, not in a pleasurable way, and I glanced away from the new friend and found Donovan standing in the doorway staring at me. My new friend, Monica, began chattering to him, telling him which food to try, unknowing at any moment he could blow. I swallowed and followed him into the family room. He was quiet, but I knew he was waiting for the opportunity to embarrass me. I didn't know how horrible it would be. Monica stood next to me, pointing out some of her friends, introducing me across the room. This adorable red hair girl wanted to be my friend and was welcoming me to their group. At one point, she yelled to her oldest friend, Desi, who was teasing her about eating all the stuffed potatoes, when Donovan blurted loudly., "No, that would be my wife, the pig." Heat coursed through my body as tears flooded my eyes. A few guys snickered and their wives elbowed them. Others said, "Not cool, Dude." Monica turned to him and said, "You're a dick. She barely ate." Donovan sneered at her, turned to her husband and pointed, "You need to control your wife."

He then dragged me from the room and out the back door, where he pulled me toward the car. He was silent on the way home; the only noise was the thumping of his thumb on the steering wheel. That night, the beating lasted longer than usual. I need to get out of this marriage?

I SHOVED THE JOURNAL BACK INTO THE BOX IN THE CLOSET; I DO not know why I'm driven to read this stuff. Jacob would never harm me. I climb into bed and wrap my arms around Jacob's waist. Eventually I slept pressed against him. My safety net. My heart.

Six

Our daughter was born on a beautiful October morning. I wish I could say her birth was painless and quick, but it wasn't. Jacob was there the entire time, holding me, helping me, and supporting me. We both cried when our daughter entered the world. A beautiful baby with my thick dark hair and Jacob's light eyes. She was the most beautiful infant in the world and very petite. She weighed slightly over six pounds. I had loved being pregnant. Everything about it, mainly because she resulted from the love I shared with Jacob. We called her Alyssa.

Jacob asked if I'd like to resign from my job to be a stay-at-home mom. We'd refinanced our home and put the proceeds from the sale of my cottage as an added down payment, and it reduced our mortgage payments drastically. It wouldn't be a hardship without my income. We weren't wealthy by any means, but we managed okay. Jacob took family leave and stayed home to help me get into a routine for the first two weeks. He was a hands-on dad, changed diapers, he did it all. I loved being a mom, loved being a stay-at-home wife, too. Jacob came home to a clean house and a fresh baby. Sometimes I may have had spit up on my shoulder, and Jacob would tease me and say, "Mommy perfume!"

One evening after the meeting, Savannah, Parker, Ruby, and I chatted in the church parking lot about the high school play we would all go to on Friday night. Jacob would be on duty, and Parker was bringing Rosie. Suddenly, the air became electrified and the hair on the back of my neck stood up. I turned to see a tall, muscular man sporting a handlebar mustache. Savannah followed my gaze and gasped, "Bart."

"Well, did you think I wouldn't find you?" He tossed an envelope at her feet. "A divorce will not stop me, you dumb bitch."

"Bart, just leave. I have a protection order." She reached for her cell phone, and he knocked it out of her hand. The screen cracked as it hit the concrete. Parker stepped up and got into his face.

"Get out of here. Now."

"Says who?"

"The police. They're on their way." He held up his phone that showed 9-1-1. Bart stepped back and reached into his jacket pocket. He pulled out a hunting knife, the blade sharp, and it shined in the moonlight. "I'll find where you live, and I'll cut you, bitch!" Bart rushed off when he heard the sirens screeching in the distance. He peeled out of the parking lot, leaving us in a dusty haze.

SEVERAL WEEKS LATER, A NEIGHBOR FOUND SAVANNAH DEAD IN her home. My best friend, the sister of my heart, was gone. The grief was unbearable as was the helplessness I felt. She had a restraining order against Bart and had moved into a gated community. The neighbors allege he was on the job and watched his estranged wife park her car and walk toward her apartment. The following day, he laid in wait and cut her throat. It was quick, vicious, and violent, leaving her to bleed to death alone in the concrete breezeway by her opened door. I knew then that I had to take things into my own hands to keep my friends safe. They released him from custody because his co-workers swore that he'd never left the job site, the building across from Savannah's. The police couldn't find his bloodied clothing or the weapon, yet Jacob and the first responders knew he did it. We knew he did it because he waited outside of one of our meetings and told her in front of a few of us, "I'll find where you live, and cut you, bitch!" He'd shown us the hunting knife. We called the police, as expected, when the police found him, he didn't have the weapon and acted like a saint. They took him in for questioning, but nothing ever came of it.

Savannah was gone, her life over before it began. Motherhood changed me; I was more protective of my friends. I imagined how I'd feel if it were my Alyssa, and it made my blood boil. Losing Savannah was like losing part of myself. We were so connected. Ruby and I cleared out her apartment. She found the designer purse Savannah and I had found at Good Will. The memories of that day flooded through me. We both grabbed it, giggling. I released it to Savannah because she worked and dressed professionally. Ruby expressed her excitement about finding a pressure cooker and teased us about the purse. She pulled the purse from the sofa, where the first responders must have tossed it. Savannah was halfway inside when Bart attacked her. Only a few more steps inside and she would have locked the door. Ruby passed me the purse. "She'd want you to have it." I nodded, tears stinging my eyes. "You two were so close, so like-minded, it's no surprise how you resembled one another." I nodded, remembering the number of people who mistook me for Savannah and her for me. We always said we were sisters separated in heaven. Ruby and I got a lot done, boxed her stuff up, and stacked it into the empty dining room. When I got home, I tossed the purse into my closet, not bothering to look inside. I just couldn't. I missed Savannah so much. My twin, my sister from another mister. After her death, an attorney reached out to me and asked me if I could come to see him. A week later, I sat alone in his office. He read Savannah's will and her wishes. I believe deep inside; she knew Bart would kill her. She left all her worldly possessions to me. Clothing, the contents of her apartment, her car and the money in the bank. It wasn't much but I donated it to the shelter for abused women. She knew I would do good with it. Everything went into storage for the next apartment our support group had to furnish.

After breaking the horrible news to her brother, Alejandro. I heard him breakdown. It was difficult to hear. He explained that he'd sent soldiers to watch over her, but they were still in flight.

It wasn't until months later that I remembered Savannah's purse. Jacob was on duty; my mother-in-law took Alyssa for a walk in her stroller. I sat on the closet floor and opened the purse. The one we both saw, and she didn't use often. Inside, a bright red wallet containing forty-two dollars, some change, a debit card, paystub, a credit card, her driver's license. Deep inside the purse in the innermost pocket, I found a blue book. I opened it and her face stared back at me. Her passport. Recently renewed. I knew her brother lived in Columbia, and she planned to visit again soon. Sobbing, I returned everything to my closet, knowing I'd never use her purse.

My husband was on many of the domestic calls and would vent to me, knowing full well how much I understood. He often passed on my information, and I'd help the victims through the process, finding them a safe place to stay. We still fostered pets when needed.

I attended church regularly and helped with the support group. It appeared the abusers got meaner, and more of them surfaced. They were a blight on society. One that bruised and spoiled the surrounding fruit. Knowing what needed to be done, I just wasn't sure how. So, I began stalking Savannah's husband to learn his routine and how I was going to take him down. I couldn't stomach blood, otherwise I'd cut his throat as he did hers. I overheard people talking about him. Calling him low life, a drinker, a thief and lazy. He gave me the Heebie-jeebies when I encountered him in town. Once at the supermarket, he whispered to me, "You look so much like my wife. I don't know what would bring me more pleasure. Fucking you or slicing your throat." The grocery store was busy and not one person looked our way, and I left without getting what I needed.

Despite Savannah's death, he didn't go back to California. He stayed behind and continued to work on the new housing development near Savannah's apartment. My stomach boiled with rage every time I saw him. I hated myself for allowing him to frighten me that day in the store.

I wished he would fall off scaffolding and die. Each time I drove by the construction zone, I whispered the word, "Die."

It came to me one sunny Saturday morning. Summer heated the road as I drove with Alyssa to support a community yard sale. Traffic teemed along leading to the neighboring town hosting a fundraiser for a terminally ill child. The community center parking lot was full, but an older man, dressed in denim overalls and a white V neck T-shirt and carrying a ladder motioned toward his truck. He pulled out, jumping the curb, so that I could pull in behind. I waved in gratitude. After exiting the car and getting Alyssa in the stroller, we perused the tables. My eyes were drawn to the item propped up against a table of tools. I knew at once it was what I needed — a sledgehammer, old, the red and yellow paint on the top mostly chipped and faded, but still heavy and useful. Ten dollars later, I had my weapon, and Alyssa had a new doll from another table. After a snack of fresh-baked cookies and juice, we left. I bought a second-hand computer at the pawnshop; I asked Pastor Robinson if I could use the small space in the basement as an office. Inside was a small kitchenette, and he told me to use whatever I needed. He could no longer climb down the steep basement steps because of his bad knees and painful hips. I offered to assist him with anything he required from downstairs. I used a computer to prepare Sunday's hymnals and sent them to the printer. They printed them and delivered them each Friday morning.

Parker, our group's only male attendee, was a school friend of Jacob's and a sweet guy. Jacob sometimes played pool or shot darts with him. I lost track of time, and our pastor informed him of my whereabouts. I secured the locker door swiftly and put the key in my jeans' pocket. I couldn't risk him seeing anything because he was so close to our family and began dating a neighbor, Rosie.

The following week, Glory cared for Alyssa while I attended the meeting. I invited her for dinner and left early for church. Before the meeting, I stored the police scanner and coffeemaker in the basement. I would begin my surveillance as soon as I could.

Since I decided on blunt force trauma using the sledgehammer. I practiced swinging it because it was massive. I bought hand weights and worked out at home. Jacob thought I wanted to build my strength, and that was true. I also told him I read that exercising released pain-relieving endorphins, also true. With practice, I could swing the heavy sledgehammer to ensure that when I made contact; it was over. Getting caught wasn't a risk I would take. Early in the mornings, I ran in the park with Alyssa in the stroller. I used to run track in school and was fast. I just haven't taken to the track since I arrived in Texas. Donovan forbade it. He beat me for merely dressing in shorts and a tank, with a thick sports bra underneath.

Two months later, the opportunity arose. My mother-in-law stayed the night because exterminators fumigated her building. I would take care of Bart on Thursday evening. He typically left the bar drunk and staggering, using most of his pay to buy drinks. Savannah often complained that he spent most of his paycheck before he got home. He'd blame her for not being able to pay their bills. Then the abuse would begin.

I left my two favorite females and hurried to church to change into the tracksuit, and I stuffed my long hair into a black knit cap. I wore a black sweatshirt, pulling the hood over the hat. All items I bought from different Good Will locations for a few mere dollars. Black latex gloves I bought at an automotive place a town over, black pants and black running shoes.

Before I left the secret room, I gloved up and walked over to the seedy bar, and I watched as daylight gave way to dusk. Bart's weapon of choice was a fifteen-inch Bowie hunting knife he carried with him in a leather sleeve. He slept with it beneath his pillow at night. I need to have the element of surprise on my side.

I almost peed my pants and threw up when I saw Bart stagger out at six thirty. I envisioned my beautiful friend Savannah and rage exploded inside me. Blinding rage. Blood pounded in my head as I snuck up behind the man who killed my best friend and swung, throwing my entire body into the swing. I almost fell with the momentum. My shoulder throbbed with pain. He went down with a thud, coppery blood flowed into a puddle as urine pooled around him. His eyes widened in the shock of death. I tossed a note on his body that said, "**Ares, the god of war, bloodshed and violence, has sought revenge. Justice is served.**"

As ANDRESSA FLED THE SCENE, TWO SOLIDLY BUILT, DARK-HAIRED men watched, their bodies pressed behind a tree. Once she disappeared, they left and called their boss.

~

I HURRIED BACK TO THE CHURCH AND ARRIVED ABOUT FIVE minutes after the meeting started. Quietly, I went to the basement to change clothes before Jacob arrived. I looked up and saw his handsome smile and felt a flutter of nerves. I quietly made my way back to him and stepped into his embrace and whispered, "Hiya, handsome!" My body trembled from fear, from what I had done. Nausea swirled in my stomach.

"Hi, my love, I can only stay a minute. I was passing by and knew you'd be here. I just needed a little sugar from my sweetie!" Jacob said. "Are you okay, babe? You're shaking."

"I'm okay. I love you so much, Jacob. Please be careful. I'd die if anything happened to you!" My nerves were getting the best of me. His job was dangerous, but I'd never been wimpy about it. I'd always thought of him being a hero, my hero.

"Honey, relax. What's bringing this on? I'll be okay, love." He was about to say something else when Parker interrupted to say hello to Jacob. The pastor called me to speak. I quickly kissed Jacob and rushed to the front. I watched Jacob leave with a wave and a wink.

After we cleaned up the meeting room, Parker followed me into the basement to put away the left-over supplies. He questioned the changes I made when I slipped the key from my pocket to open the padlock that I had placed on the door.

"I'm helping Pastor Robinson." My mouth was dry, and I licked my lips. I heard the thump from the sledgehammer as it hit his head in my mind. "With clerical stuff. He gave me this space to use as an office." Parker nodded, placated. "Go on home. Thanks for helping bring the supplies down here. I need to place an order with the printer for next week's services." My eyes were fixed on him as he placed the brewer in the sink. "I'll clean that. You head home, Parker."

"Sure thing. Don't go home too late. I can wait if you'd like.

I'm heading to Rosie's tonight, spending the night!" He rocked on his heels; his happiness was palpable.

"Unnecessary, Jacob swings by to watch as I get to the car. Marry that girl. She's a keeper!" I lied about Jacob. He assumed I left with Parker after each meeting, knowing he helped me clean up. I turned the interior lock into place slowly as I heard Parker's tread on the steps. I washed the sledgehammer in the deep sink and poured oxygenated cleaner on it, rinsed, and dried it. Shoved it back in the cabinet and locked it up.

Finally, at home, I checked on Alyssa. Making my way down the hallway, I climbed into our empty bed and tried to sleep, hugging Jacob's pillow, but mostly paced and pleaded for my soul the entire night. I'm flawed, and I know it, but I feel the urge to help the helpless, and ridding them of the abusers is the only way I know how. God, forgive me!

HEARTBROKEN, ALEJANDRO DIDN'T LEAVE HIS OFFICE FOR DAYS after learning of his sister's death. He didn't learn soon enough that Bart found her; he knew he should have killed the evil son of a bitch years ago. But he made a promise to his sister. Now she was gone, her throat cut by her piece of shit husband. His phone was ringing, and the name Hugo appeared on his private phone. "Yes, Hugo?"

"Well, we stuck around to get vengeance on Savannah's former husband. But ... someone else did the deed."

"Someone else? Who?"

"Andressa Swanson, Savannah's best friend. She killed Bart."

He disconnected the call to make another. "Yes?"

"I have a job for you." Alejandro explained what he needed, how much he will pay, and after finalizing his contract, the man known only as the observer, set his plan in motion. His routine in fresh cases was to gather intel on routines. He headed to

Texas and within a day, bought an older motor home and arrived in Clayton Heights.

∾

ALYSSA DRANK HER MORNING BOTTLE IN MY ARMS WHEN JACOB walked in the door after his shift. Glory went for her morning walk. He took one look at me and knew something was wrong. "Honey, what's wrong? You look upset." Of course, I was upset, afraid to turn on the news, which I usually watched on the small kitchen television. "I had a painful night and bad dreams when I finally fell asleep. I've been up since two."

"Oh sweetheart, perhaps mom can take care of Alyssa this morning, and you can get a few hours of sleep with me. I'm going to hop in the shower before bed. The air conditioner in the cruiser wasn't working, and I feel nasty.

"That sounds like a good idea. I'll ask mom when she gets back from her walk."

"Ask me what, Andi?" My mother-in-law said as she stepped inside.

"Jacob suggested asking you to care for Alyssa for a few hours; I had a rough, painful night and got little sleep." Although I was always in pain, I hated lying about the reason I was so upset.

"Of course, sweetheart, go get some sleep. Take meds for pain too. I thought something was wrong. You seemed down and not your normal cheerful self. Whenever you need me, you just call. I love my family and am here to help!"

Tears burned my eyes and threatened to spill down my cheeks when she hugged and kissed me. What am I doing? I could destroy this beautiful family that I have. I made breakfast and had it ready for Jacob when he returned, and he was always so appreciative. "Thanks, hon, smells delicious."

I lost control of my emotions and tears poured down my

face. I sobbed over the kitchen sink. Jacob rushed over and said, "I'll clean up, honey. Take something for the pain and get into bed."

I overheard my mother-in-law say, "Go to her. I'll clean up. Maybe it's hormones. They're rough on a new mom. Things are trying to get back to normal in her body. She's like the energizer bunny around here. I've never seen such a devoted wife and mother. Go, Jacob! I'll take care of my granddaughter. Bless her heart."

Jacob entered the bedroom quietly. I lay on my side of the bed, my pillow soaked with tears. He stripped down to his underwear and climbed into bed, spooning me. He caressed my head gently and whispered into my ear. "It's okay, honey, I'm here, and I promise never to let anything happen to you. I know that the support group sometimes makes you sad and angry, and I also know it's what you need to do. But it's okay to take a break. Would you like to go home and see your family? We can take care of things here."

I couldn't answer; the guilt was overwhelming. I turned around to face Jacob. "I'll think about it. Thank you."

I leaned over and gently kissed his lips. We made love, and I fell asleep in Jacob's arms. Making love to Jacob always made me feel better, and it was still tender, passionate, and loving. I woke up after lunch, my stomach growling. The house was quiet as Alyssa napped. Glory sat by the pool, dipping her feet in the warm water. I sat beside her, noticing the baby monitor on the patio table. "Thanks, Mom. I appreciate everything you do for us."

"I know you do, Andi, and I appreciate what a wonderful wife you are to my son. A lot of my friends don't have daughters-in-law like you. I'm blessed and always feel welcome around you."

"Mom, I love you. You created the most wonderful man, and I love him so much. I'm grateful to be blessed with a wonderful mom like you." I squeezed her hand. "Jacob offered me the opportunity to go home to see my family, and I think I'd like to take Alyssa. Would you like to join me? I'd love to take you to see the popular tourist sites."

"Oh gee, sweetie, I've never been on a plane before. But I'd like to go with you."

"Then it's a plan. Let's schedule it for Jacob's next overnight shift. That's the shift when he works all night and sleeps most of the day. I normally only get to see him a few hours a day. I'll grab his calendar." Inside, I pulled his calendar from the refrigerator. I brought the calendar outside, and we decided that in three weeks, we'd leave for New York. I borrowed Jacob's tablet and booked the flights. After calling my brother, he invited us to stay with him in his new house.

When Jacob woke up later that day, Alyssa drank her bottle in my arms when Jacob walked in the kitchen, while my mother-in-law watched her game show in the den. He took one look at me and knew something was wrong. "Honey, what's wrong? You still look upset."

Of course, I was still upset. I'm still afraid to turn on the five o'clock news, which I usually watch on the small kitchen television while I prepare dinner. "I'm in a lot of pain. Don't worry, Jacob, it will pass." He isn't used to me complaining about pain. I keep it to myself, but I had to justify the tears somehow. Truly, I am not a bad person. I wiped my tears and stood.

Jacob scanned my face. Other than holding me, he didn't know how to ease my pain. He kissed me and reassured me of his love.

Tears burned my eyes and threatened to spill down my cheeks when I rushed to him and wrapped my arms around him. He turned to me and kissed my forehead and made his way to the bathroom. Glory reached around and hugged me from behind. *What am I doing? I could destroy this beautiful family that I have.* I finished dinner and had it ready for Jacob when he returned, and he was always grateful.

After dinner, I cut Jacob a thick slice of pie, his favorite blueberry, when Callie promptly jumped on his lap for love. As he caressed her, he said, "Oh, I forgot to tell you, honey, Savannah's ex-husband was found dead last night at the bar. They initially thought he collapsed in a drunken stupor until they found a note."

I turned my face toward the sink and washed Alyssa's bottles. "A note, honey?" I asked, my mouth dry, and my heart raced. I could feel the trembling begin in my stomach. A nauseating bout of doubt permeated. *Are they onto me?*

"Not sure, I wasn't on the call, was in the precinct eating lunch—that amazing lasagna you made, babe. If I remember correctly, it said something about war and revenge. Something about the god of war. It's in evidence. It was a busy morning, an accident at Devil's Curve, too." He reminded her that there were a lot of accidents on that road. The sharp curves paralleled a ravine with a deep and gushing waterway about a hundred feet below. Drivers sped through, almost as though the devil was chasing them. Rarely did the bodies resurface, and other times, they were lost forever. The currents were swifter in the choppy channel of the curve. They commonly knew the road as Devil's Mountain or Curve, depending on which side of the road you lived on.

I quickly gulped a glass of water to distract myself and Jacob. Thankfully, Callie was demanding and wanted her daddy's attention because I heard him say, "Callie, you're such a needy girl. I guess you're not getting enough love from Daddy since Alyssa came." She loved it and purred, adoring the attention.

I couldn't take my mind off my best friend. Savannah thought she'd found her one and only at nineteen. Instead, she found herself married to a man who beat her and threatened to cut her throat. Her story was typical of most abusive relationships. He trapped her, and she kept the trauma secret from her only living relative back in Columbia. Her brother Alejandro.

Their relationship started with promises of a better life and adoration. It quickly moved to isolation and extreme manipulation. Then horror, the violence, is what nightmares were made of.

To gather strength and the reason I need to do this, I read my journals. One significant thing I learned was that trauma triggers often affected the survivor. For me, it was true, and they come in many forms. Triggers are personal in nature. Just about anything can trigger a survivor. My personal triggers are flashbacks. Certain words could be a trigger, even Jacob unknowingly could trigger me if he had a rough day. He'd raise his voice, not at me, just explaining his day. I thought after being single for two years, I'd gotten over the triggers, but they come at random times. I cried and shook if I smelled someone who used the same cologne or after shave as Donovan. It was a common brand and not unique to Donovan, yet it caused an anxiety attack or a full-blown panic attack. I often wondered if they were the same thing.

Later that week, Jacob surprised me with a long weekend at Disney, with Glory and Alyssa. We flew and several hours later we checked into the hotel; it was hard not to be happy in the "happiest place on earth". Although Alyssa was so young, her face lit up with the colorful attractions and the music. Later that night, the hotel delivered Alyssa's crib and set it up in Glory's room, which adjoined ours. Jacob was attentive, and we made love several times. It was like he couldn't get enough of me. He was always so gentle, and I loved that about him. It was as though he worshiped my body. Never once did he call attention to my post pregnancy stretch marks. He kissed them and touched them tenderly.

We ate all the meals in the park and I knew this was probably an enormous hit to our budget, but he didn't mind. He claimed it was something he wanted to do to make me happy. His very presence made me joyful. One night Glory feigned exhaustion and insisted we go to dinner alone. We stayed close by but enjoyed an amazing meal in a local steakhouse. Jacob loved a good steak, and I enjoyed red meat occasionally. The restaurant was a colorful Brazilian steakhouse, and the Gauchos brought meats on skewers that were cooked on an open fire. We enjoyed a salad beforehand and Jacob was ready to tuck into the meats offered. Round and round the servers appeared with fresh cuts. I turned my wooden block red while Jacob continued to enjoy the meats cooked on an open flame. Jacob was in a food coma by the time we left. Later that night, we discussed having another baby. It wasn't like we used protection, but Jacob actively wanted to focus on getting pregnant. We made love so many times on that vacation, I could barely walk. But in a good way. The vacation took my mind off everything. For a brief time, I forgot I was married before him. I forgot the evil. Jacob was perfect, at least to me, he was.

AUGUST 5

TONIGHT, WE WENT TO A FORMAL PARTY AT A HOTEL. MISS SHIRLEY, my mother-in-law, took me shopping for a gown. After trying on several, she admitted the emerald- green sequined gown looked stunning. It had long sleeves, a V-neck, and hung to the floor with a slight train. Honestly, I felt like a princess wearing it. It needed to be taken in at the waist, but everything else was perfect. The seamstress told me not to lose any weight. I wasn't trying, but Donovan often made my plate. Mere morsels. It was all about control and not kindness.

I felt pretty when we left the house. As usual, Donovan said nothing. When we arrived, Miss Shirley made a fuss over me, introducing me to her friends. Even my normal stoic Father-in-law told me how beautiful I looked. Donovan stood near the exit most of the evening. Drinking. A lot. His mother kept me by her side. We sat at his parents' table. If it weren't for Donovan's scowl, he'd look handsome. I was grateful not to be in his orbit. He sat next to me when dinner was served. A beautiful Kobe Wagyu steak. His mom bragged about how delicious it was and they cooked it to perfection. I was about four bites in when Donovan told me to stop. I placed my fork beside my plate and my hands in my lap, fighting tears.

My mother-in-law whispered. "Don't you like it, dear? "I told her it was delicious. Most of the women were eating the steak and enjoying it. "Enjoy it, dear, it's okay, all the ladies will eat the entire piece." I tucked in, mimicking my mother-in-law's tiny bites. I guess she thought I was trying to maintain my weight. If only. Donovan's attention was on his father and didn't realize I disobeyed him until the servers removed the plates. He leaned over, his hot breath against my cheek. "You'll pay, bitch. " It didn't matter that I didn't touch the loaded baked potato. I ate the meat, against his orders. I knew why. He wanted to finish it despite his weight being out of control. His former six pack changed into a dad's body and now a huge nine-month pregnant woman's belly. His face rounded, and he grew a beard that he only groomed to see his parents.

Once at home, he shoved me to the kitchen table, lifted my dress, and pulled my undergarments down. "You ate like a pig tonight." Now I am going to stick you like a pig. Every time I push into you, you are to oink like the pig that you are." He shoved himself inside. When I didn't make a noise, he grabbed my hair in his fist and yanked my head back so far that I thought he'd break my neck. I wanted to die, but I also wanted to escape and live like a normal girl in her twenties. After I felt my hair being ripped from my scalp, I made the noise. How much more can I take? How can I let this continue?

. . .

AUGUST 6

MY HEAD HURTS SO BADLY. I DON'T KNOW WHAT TO DO. I NEVER imagined I would become a woman who would fall victim to this behavior. Physical, emotional and verbal abuse. I'm worn out.

AUGUST 16

DONOVAN IS STILL OINKING WHEN HE COMES HOME. HE THINKS HE'S funny. I called him an asshole under my breath. He heard me and attacked me. I'm now sporting a black and blue eye. It's swollen shut.

AUGUST 30

DONOVAN CAME HOME FROM WORK IN A FOUL MOOD. WELL, MORE foul than usual.

He blames me for the lack of funds to move some place better. He tapped the newspaper ad showing the new apartments down the road. I offered, yet again, to get a job. I tried cajoling him. "Maybe if I went to work, we could get a nice place with a fire-place, remarking on the photo his finger rested on. He started again about how I will not leave this house to go to a job. "You want a fireplace, pig? " He rolled up the newspaper, lit it on the stove and dropped it on the kitchen floor engulfed in flames and walked out the door! I used my cheap tennis shoes to stomp on it.

My sneakers melted, and I burned the bottom of my feet. My neighbor Lisa smelled the smoke and tended to my feet.

OCTOBER 22

I'M SO TIRED OF THIS LIFE. WHAT DID I DO TO DESERVE THIS? Donovan came home with a gun. For protection. He stuck it in his nightstand. I'm even more afraid.

OCTOBER 29

TODAY WAS MY FIRST SUPPORT MEETING FOR WOMEN SUFFERING through spousal abuse. Thankfully, Donovan didn't know that I left the house. Afraid to speak but listened and learned. How could I not trigger him when my very existence annoyed him? I wanted to die.

Seven

The blaring phone interrupted Rod Jackson's morning routine. He had the San Antonio Press opened to the sports page and his coffee in a cardboard cup on top of the dingy gray desk. He reached for it, swallowing the bite of the breakfast sandwich he'd just shoved into his mouth. "Lieutenant Jackson, what can I do for you?"

"Rod, it's Chuck."

"Chuckie, how are you, buddy?" Sheriff Edwards and Rod were in the academy together and twenty-five years later, and they were still good friends.

"I could be better. There's a situation over here. I need your help." Rod listened and gathered his keys while he listened to the story. He reached for his notebook and stuffed it into his breast pocket.

"Chuck, I'm on my way now. Don't let anyone contaminate the scene."

"Secured buddy, see ya soon." Chuck looked at his watch, knowing it could take about an hour with traffic. He turned to his deputy. "CSU is on the way." Chuck watched the main road, waiting for the medical examiner to arrive. The smell of stale beer and urine accosted his nostrils. Beneath him was Bart Cruz, his head split open, blood following a trail, pooling in the cracked concrete. The victim lay in a puddle of his urine.

No one liked Bart, except maybe his cronies and the like, but not the townspeople. They were grateful when he moved to California. He was mean drunk and even meaner sober. When they learned of his former wife's murder, everyone suspected he killed her. Chuck knew he'd get nowhere with the people of Clayton Heights. They'd be relieved to see that he was dead. Chuck took in his surroundings, waiting for Rod to arrive from San Antonio. He noticed lights approaching in the distance as the medical examiner's van pulled into the lot and walked around back to where Bart lay. Sheriff Charles Edwards held the note he'd carefully placed into an evidence bag.

The M.E. examined the body and looked at Sheriff Edwards, who shook his head. "Not yet, Doc. Waiting on CSU, coming in from San Antonio."

Rod arrived fifty minutes later and hustled to the scene. "What'd ya got?"

"Thirty-six-year-old male, deceased, appears to have been bludgeoned."

"Witnesses?"

"Not a one."

"Cameras?"

"Out here?" Chuck snorted. "The bar doesn't have them, and there's nothing else around."

Rod surveyed the area, the blue rusted metal door that the victim used, his motorcycle parked in the rear. "Does everyone use that door?" Rod pointed.

"Nah, just him. He walks through the kitchen. Everyone else uses the front door and parks in the lot by the road. Bart thought he was special and parked out here. He's special alright, serves him right, now he's lying in a puddle of his own piss."

Surprised by the venom, Rod asked, "You are?"

"Jed, owner of The Watering Hole. I bought it when I got back from 'Nam."

"What do you know about him?" He peered at the bar; the old brick building sat alone on the stretch of highway.

"He's a murdering son of a bitch, murdered that sweet girl, he did. I know it, we all know it, yet he got off. It looks like someone took out the trash." He snorted.

"And who do you think did that?"

"Don't know, but I'd buy him a drink, that's for damn sure!"

"Where were you when he left?"

"Behind the bar, like always. Ask anybody. Bart left around nine, drank since three. His typical Friday behavior."

Rod interviewed everyone and came up with nothing. This was the most intensive investigation the Sheriff's department has ever attempted. Frustrated, he headed back to San Antonio and home. His wife, Jolie, was bending over the oven, checking dinner. Rod playfully swatted her backside.

"Hey, Freshie!" Jolie responded to the swat, "You're late, I have a roaster on warm."

"Sorry cutie. I spent the afternoon in Clayton Heights, murder case," he mentioned as he sat at his place setting and ran his hands through his hair.

"You're exhausted. Eat, and I'll clean up tonight. You relax. I bought you a bag of the kettle corn you like."

"The best wifey ever!"

They finished dinner, cleaned the kitchen, Jolie sat on the sofa and asked, "Anything you need to discuss?" Jolie was a retired police officer; she took early retirement when she found a lump and the doctor diagnosed her with breast cancer. She has been in remission but prefers to be at home. The chemo and radiation changed her, weakened her, and she doubted her capabilities as an officer.

"Nah, I want to watch TV. Maybe after I investigate more, we'll brainstorm. I just want to chill with you and the terrors," he said, referring to the two rescue pit bulls cuddled on the love seat. "How are you today, cutie?"

"Good, took the babies for a walk. Layla is getting so much better on the leash."

"She's probably learning from Tank." Rod watched TV in the comfortable family room. Jolie decorated the room with leather furniture and cozy pillows. He looked at the walls they painted together when they first bought the place. She wanted tan walls. It needed repainting, but neither had the energy. She because of chemo, he because of working long hours.

The Clayton Heights Times

FRIDAY, OCTOBER 29, 2007

BREAKING NEWS
The latest local News
-James Nilson

BODY FOUND BEHIND LOCAL BAR.
Bright yellow police tape surrounds the Watering Hole, a local bar on Route 42. The police confirmed they received a call to the rear of the establishment where the body was located.

They have identified the victim as Bart Cruz, 36, of Los Angeles. Cruz was pronounced dead on the scene at 9:15 PM by the Clayton County Coroner. This suspicious death is under investigation. Cruz is the former husband of the late Savannah Cruz, who was found murdered at her home two months ago. It was alleged that Mr. Cruz was involved. A Watering Hole representative stated he did not know until he went outside with trash and found the body. We expect the local police to release additional details in the morning.

Eight

The holiday season arrived, and the local shops decorated West Avenue, which was our primary thoroughfare through town. Most of the shops jointly decorated the small avenue in bright lights, Santas, and snowmen. We often walked around with Alyssa in the evenings. The fresh air seemed to encourage a good night's sleep. Her bright eyes widened at the lights, and she'd point at the colorful lights making baby noises. If Jacob was on shift, Glory often went with me. We'd stop at the coffee shop and get whatever fancy flavor of the day was served.

February came with little change to the mild temperatures. Alyssa was growing. She was a happy baby, and I enjoyed being a mother. One evening, in the middle of the month, our meeting began without one of our members, Augusta. It wasn't unheard of, but we worried because her husband had recently threatened her.

Augustina Lambourne lived in a small bungalow three blocks north from the church. When she promised to bake her mother's famous pound cake and she hadn't shown up for the weekly meeting, we knew something was wrong. Our phone calls went unanswered. I called Jacob, who went to do a safety check. On his way, he encountered the local volunteer fire fighters speeding down the road toward her house. We all heard the sirens and thought there was a car accident unrelated to Augustina. The house was on fire, and it had partially burned Augustina by the time Jacob arrived. She died from the gunshot wound to her chest. They found her body in the foyer, the cake on an entry table, along with her car keys. Thankfully, her teenage son was at his grandmother's house. Neighbors saw her former husband Phillip running from the scene, minutes after they saw the smoke. The police issued an APB out on him.

Jacob talked to me after his shift. The police found Phillip's mother, but his parents said he took cash and ran away. The police had visited their home several times. They learned the next day of their daughter-in-law's death. I remembered Augustina mentioning a hunting cabin in the woods off Edgemont Road. Lots of hunters had small roughly construed cabins, others had hunting stands built into the trees. She mentioned it was a one-room log cabin, the only one. Her husband, shortly after the divorce, kept her captive inside for two weeks. *If only I could find it.* My memory wasn't as good as it used to be, thanks again to Donovan. Phillip released her after meeting someone else. Another woman foolishly believed in his smooth talking. That was Phillip, according to Augustina, a smooth talker. Snake oil salesmen. A user with a short fuse. She told me the cabin was supposed to be a weekend getaway for them. Instead, he took her there to cook and clean while he played hunter in the woods. I needed to find that cabin. After weeks of surveillance, I spotted Phillip. He grew a beard and shaved his head, but it was him. I then planned his demise.

I read a few more journal entries to call on my inner goddess. This one was at a company picnic at a local park.

· · ·

I'm dressed in Bermuda shorts and a company T-shirt, cheap white sneakers I bought from the grocery store for $3.99. My hair is in a ponytail. The only comment Donovan made was for me to behave because he had easy access to my hair. Mental note to self: cut it off! I refused to get food, despite the mouthwatering barbecue smells coming from inside the tents. My mother-in-law looked lovely in a denim sundress. She stayed close by. When she saw I wasn't eating, she brought me a plate. I sat next to her and my father-in-law while Donovan eyed the single girls. My mother-in-law wanted a piece of cake and asked me to walk with her. I refused a slice but held onto hers while she filled a bowl with fruit. Donovan walked over and oinked. He pushed the plate into my face in front of everyone. He stalked away, snickering. I saw his father grab his arm, but he pulled away. He left, and I went home with my in-laws and spent the night there.

The following morning, my father-in-law took me home on his way to work. I knew by now Donovan left. I opened the door, grateful for a few hours reprieve. Except he grabbed me and slammed the door. He sexually assaulted me. Broke two of my fingers and the punch that landed on my lip, cut it. My lips swelled immediately.

THREE WEEKS LATER, THE SUN PEEKED THROUGH THE CLOUDS AS I climbed out of bed. Alyssa lay on her back, chewing on her stuffed bear's foot. After changing her diaper, I brought her into the kitchen to feed her breakfast. Jacob was in a class and then had to qualify to keep his sharpshooter status. He'd be out of town the entire day. Glory would arrive shortly to watch Alyssa. I had errands and was eager to get a run in. After Glory arrived, I drove to the park to run. After running along the small track, I slipped out of the back entrance and ran a mile to Edgemont Road. It wasn't uncommon to see runners on this road early in the mornings or after dinner because it wasn't heavily traveled. Fortunately, only one tractor trailer blew by me so fast it felt like the breeze would knock me down. He clearly didn't see me running alongside the road. With trepidation, I followed a well-worn path into the woods where I found the cabin, but it was on the other side of the lake. *Did Edgemont circle around? I'm sure Augusta told me it was Edgemont.* I turned around and went home, planning to try again another day.

Later in the week, after grocery shopping Alyssa dozed in her car seat, I drove down Edgemont and found the turn. I followed the turn and saw the entrance to state park owned property, but not a private road. Pickup trucks with gun racks lined the road. I slowed down but didn't see any humans. Just dense woods. I'd try again without Alyssa.

I slipped out to keep the house quiet for Jacob. He had just come off the third shift and was exhausted. These shifts were the hardest for him with a baby at home, one who just found her voice. So off to Glory's we went. Most days it was like a mini vacation. We'd go to the park, have lunch, and do some shopping. Sometimes I ran errands while Alyssa slept. We bought a small playpen and set it up in Glory's bedroom.

I drove to Edgemont Road and found a small dirt road to the left of the state park's entrance and parked half a mile away, hidden in the woods. I jogged to the cabin and waited out by the lake. Phillip fished by the lake. I waited until he sat comfortably on the tiny hunting stool. Stealthily, I made my way toward him and swung the sledgehammer with all my might. It sounded like the crack of his skull floated across the lake and reverberated across the silence of the forest. The blood bubbled through the gash in his head, and I gagged.

He attempted to turn to see what had happened. Blood flowed quickly from the gash. Instead, his head moved to the left, partly from the impact and, I assumed, partly from the damage to his brain. He fell sideways and landed in the lake, almost as though he dove in, smooth, almost graceful with extraordinarily little ripples in the water. I expected an enormous splash. I dropped the note on the hunting stool and ran, taking the route I used to get there. **Nemesis, goddess of revenge and balance. Justice is served.** I hurried to the church and slipped downstairs to the office to change.

THE SPY FALLS BEHIND THE HONDA, INTENT ON LEARNING THE next target. He's in the cheap car he bought two towns over for cash. It's an older ordinary Toyota, and it runs well. The car is nothing like the fancy SUV he drives at home. This car is inconspicuous and fits in. He's cars behind the silver Honda driven by Andressa. She turns and heads east toward the Clayton Heights Nature Reserve. His heart races when he sees her hazard lights turn on, then quickly turn off. Almost as though she didn't mean to put them on. She exited the car and opened the trunk; her back was to him. He watched as she tucked the weapon into her pants and covered her hair with a knit cap and pulled the hood from her sweatshirt over it. His heart pumps against his ribcage as he follows her into the dense foliage. His breathing is steady as he walks almost parallel to her. He notices the man at the same time she did. He's sitting on a canvas stool, fishing. Andressa swings, the blow hits his temple. He goes down almost gracefully, landing seamlessly into the lake. She drops something on the stool and sprints back. He waited a beat before leaving and covering her tracks with his before heading back to his car.

As Andressa fled the scene, the thick, dark-haired man pressed his body into the tree. Once she cleared the tree line, he followed in her footsteps, his huge boot-steps overlaying hers.

Two days later, she is in the grocery store as the Observer puts cereal into his cart. He waves to the little girl seated in the buggy as her mother chooses a healthy cereal. He felt a trickle of sweat slip down his face. His heart raced and blood flowed south when she offered him a smile. It's been a long time since he felt an attraction to a woman, much less a client. A killer.

Their shopping trip is in a strange sync as each aisle he needs she is in. He follows his list and pretends to be occupied with it. He prepares and eats most of his food in the RV. Every now and again, he'll grab take out.

Once he hears of an abusive situation, he'll know who will be next. He searches for a police scanner and learns there is an app. He downloaded it on his phone and set the area. Listening to the app during his free time, when he knows his target is safely ensconced in her home, proves useful. Other times he reads, enjoying the downtime. Not having grown up with a television, he doesn't miss it. Even though there is a small TV mounted on the wall of the motor home.

Returning home, I ran inside and showered, sat on the shower floor, and cried. *Am I insane? It's destroying me inside, yet I can't allow another woman to suffer.*

When Jacob asked why my face was blotchy, I merely replied. "I had a painful night. When I finally fell asleep, I had a nightmare. I've been up since two."

"Nightmare, sweetheart? About Donovan?" I nodded as tears stung my eyes. He pulled me into his embrace. "It's okay baby, I've got you. He can't hurt you. No one will hurt you on my watch. I promise you."

"I know Jacob. You would never hurt me. I think sometimes I'm damaged." *It's this dark inner goddess, is what I don't say.* "My mind remembers everything so vividly and I panic. It's not so bad when you are next to me."

"You understand with my job that's not always a possibility?"

"Oh sweetheart, I understand. I just wanted you to know it doesn't happen all the time. You are my safe place. I guess that's why I don't freak out when you are home."

Nine

Rod was still at home, nursing his coffee. He planned on heading back to Clayton Heights to interview people in town regarding the Cruz murder. His phone vibrated on the kitchen table, the loud ringtone frightening the dog. He reached for it. "Yeah?"

"We got another body." He hurried to Clayton Heights, using back roads to avoid the rush hour traffic. He found the cabin and the police activity after a long hike into the woods, having parked in the wrong location. Sweating profusely, he arrived and found the Sheriff. "Chuck, what the hell is going on? What's your gut saying?"

"Revenge. Vigilante. I'm not sure. You know we don't experience this kind of crime."

"Yeah buddy, I know." He eyed the perimeter. "M.E. get here yet?"

"Yeah, he's examining now. We taped off the area. Let's go." Rod followed his friend around the small wooden cabin to the shoreline. The water gently lapped at the sand as the wind blew. Rod sneezed violently into his handkerchief. After a brief discussion with the M.E., he headed into the cabin for clues. He turned toward the police officer, "Hey officer, can you check for hunting cameras?" Chuck followed him inside the one-room cabin. On the far-left wall is a full-sized bed, its tarnished brass headboard against the wall. One wooden nightstand with a small oil lamp sat beneath the narrow window. He opened the door behind the bed and found a small closet and a tiny bathroom. The kitchen sat at the far right, with an old wooden table with four mismatched chairs. An old stove, a microwave, and a small refrigerator. Inside the cabinet, he found plastic dishes with mis-matched coffee mugs. Discount store stuff. The food was typical of a man's space: canned goods, beef jerky, and junk food. Easy. Chuck watched Rod silently as he took notes. When Rod gazed at him, he said, "What have you got for me?"

"We found his wife Augustina shot in her foyer. They expected her at the church for the support group. They alerted the police when she didn't show up. One of my officers found the house ablaze and a gunshot wound to her chest. A fatal shot."

"What support group?"

"For abused women."

"Think they're involved in this?"

"No way! They are good people, churchgoers. They just gather to support one another."

"I need a list of the attendees. All of them. Regulars and anyone who attends."

"Rod dude, of course, but you're wasting your time on them."

"Still need the information, sooner rather than later." Chuck nodded and hiked back to his car. He followed the M.E. and the other officers with the body. Hours later, Chuck faxed the list over to Rod in San Antonio.

Surprised to learn that not one of the town's residents is calling the police asking where they were with the investigation. Not even the mayor has called. Chuck often received calls about neighbors barking dogs. But not one call about the murders. Not. One.

Rod's car ate up the miles as he headed back to Clayton Heights. He drives while creating a mental picture of the previous scenes and the questions he wants answered. He turns off the car ignition outside the first house on his list of interviewees. After interviewing each member of the support group. Parker McCully at his job, Ruby Miller at home, Pastor Ezekiel Robinson at the Church and Andressa Swanson at home with her baby daughter. He pulled out his bound regulation notebook and jotted down notes for each interview. He knew that if this went to court, the attorney would ask for his notebook.

Later, back in the office, he perused his field notes:

1:45 PM

Parker McCully: Met him on the Job, (Hayes Industries) 1200 Branch Road, a quietly positive individual. Seems like a straight up guy. Didn't fidget. Mother was a victim of abuse by his stepfather. The stepfather's been gone for over fifteen years. Was at home with his girlfriend last night. Rosie Jonas of Clayton Heights. Although quiet, he was confident in his answers. Didn't know the victim.

Ruby Miller: Home interview. 1405 Piney Glenn. knocked on her door. She was cheerful and sociable. Was at the movies with a neighbor. The small theater on Main Street saw Gone with the Wind with Theodore Garcia. Didn't know the victim. Admitted that she didn't care if the unsub was caught, "He is ridding the town of waste."

. . .

ANDRESSA SWANSON: HOME INTERVIEW. 1602 GREENBANK Drive. Married to a local police officer, Jacob Swanson. Was at home with her mother-in-law, Glory Swanson and her baby. Jacob stopped in for dinner during his shift. No need to follow up. She was articulate and spoke of her friends. Didn't know their spouses. She seemed nervous because the baby was fussy.

PASTER EZEKIEL ROBINSON: CLAYTON HEIGHT WESLEYAN Church. 1500 Herbert Rd. Someone had set up a Bingo game in the small room where the groups usually meet. He enjoys being among the congregation and the sweets they bring. He is a man of small stature and seems like a gentle soul.

ROD TYPED HIS NOTES INTO A REPORT AND SLID THEM INTO A folder. Confident that these people weren't guilty of anything. He reached out to Chuck, "Yo Buddy. I'm back in San Antonio. Can you check to see if there are any nature cameras out by the Lambourne cabin? We might not see the murder, but someone might stand out."

"Buddy, it's old school. I doubt it, but I'll check myself." This section of woods is owned by a local man, long decease who sold parcels off to friends, who built rough hunting or fishing cabins. The cabin the Lambourne's owned was in Phillip's family for decades.

The Clayton Heights Times

WEDNESDAY, MARCH 27, 2007

BREAKING NEWS
The latest local News
-James Nilson

FIRE FIGHTERS WERE CALLED TO A HOUSE FIRE ON WILD OAK Road. Flames and smoke spread throughout the area and were visible for miles. Volunteer firefighters arrived in minutes where they found a Clayton Heights woman's body inside her burning home last night. Next of kin identified the victim as Augustina Lambourne. Police have confirmed she was already deceased by a gunshot wound to the chest when they arrived. The fire is still under investigation, but they quoted the fire chief as saying he was confident an accelerant caused it. The county coroner confirmed that the gunshot was the apparent cause of death. Neighbors claim they saw Phillip Lambourne enter the house and several minutes later, he ran out. Heading north as smoke billowed from beneath the front door. Police want Lambourne for questioning.

Ten

Our trip to New York was beautiful, and we did a lot of fun things with my parents. My mother-in-law and my parents got along as though they'd been friends for years. Glory particularly loved the boat ride to the Statue of Liberty. She felt like she touched history, climbing the steps inside the statue. Of course, we took her to the Empire State Building, too. We walked on Fifth Avenue. I learned Glory was a fashionista in her day. She promised to show me pictures. My father took time off and went to the tourist traps with us, because he wanted to spend every minute with me and his granddaughter. Alyssa was so well behaved and always in her Papa's arms. She tweaked his nose with her saliva coated hands. She was teething and her hands were always in her mouth.

Glory enjoyed New York and the unique foods and cultures but was eager to get home to the quiet of our little town.

I was sad to leave, but I was eager to see Jacob. I missed him so.

The next year went by so fast. Alyssa had just celebrated her second birthday when I learned I was pregnant again. Jacob and

I were thrilled. The pregnancy was uneventful, and our little son was born much quicker than Alyssa.

Jacob Swanson, Jr., who we would call Jake, was a delightful baby. As easy as Alyssa to care for, Jacob and I were so in love with our babies. Our family.

I got back into the swing of things with the group. It was a peaceful time for our members. My husband and mother-in-law were both incredibly supportive. Eventually, we invited Jacob's mom to move in with us. Her apartment rent had gone up to an unaffordable amount for a woman with a small pension and social security. We had an ample house, and even if we became parents again, there would still be plenty of room. It was difficult for me to help much with the move with two babies, but most afternoons, I have them nap at Grandma's, and she and I would pack up what we could. She planned to donate her furniture to abused women starting over. She just asked if she could take her rocker; it was a piece that her husband bought when she became pregnant with Jacob. Jacob placed it by the window, facing the television in the family room.

When Jake was eight months old, one of our members, Georgia Stevens' estranged husband, Alan, viciously attacked her. Yet again, the restraining order failed her. Alan Stevens was a prominent criminal attorney, and he influenced the minds of the system. Ironic that he was a criminal himself. How could anyone be held accountable when he himself paid off whoever he could to keep his antics away from Clayton Heights? But I learned of them, Alan Stevens, prominent attorney, had a secret. The man enjoyed prostitutes and frequented them often. They caught him three times, with his pants down, involved in sexual acts. He enjoyed the young male prostitutes. I only knew because I overheard a conversation at the police station when I delivered Jacob's forgotten lunch. The entire conversation happened unknowing that I was sitting on the other side of the cubicle.

OVER TWO YEARS LATER, THE SCANNER WENT OFF WITH something of interest to the observer. Police and rescue were called to the home of Georgia Stevens. The observer listened. He followed Andressa and learned that the woman's husband, Alan Stevens, put his wife in the hospital and she suffered a traumatic brain injury because of his beating. He knew who was next and made sure he stuck close to Andressa.

After he gathered his gear and shoved it into the trunk, he began surveillance, and just as he expected, Andressa began stalking Mr. Stevens.

WE'D MOVED GEORGIA OUT OF THE SHELTER AND INTO A ONE-bedroom apartment within walking distance of the church. She found a job as a receptionist with a local primary care physician. Happily adjusting to being single when someone brutally attacked her in the parking lot of the grocery store. She survived the attack, but the doctors stated that she would be permanently disabled and required a long recovery. We took turns sitting vigil by her bedside, sheltering her with our love and protection. I took the shift from seven to midnight, after my babies were in bed. Some nights, Jacob sat with me so that we could spend time together. Once they released her, she stayed with another member, Ruby, the same woman I stayed with all those years ago.

I went to the church office and paced, thinking of ways to get this guy caught. I didn't want to have to take this on. The last one almost killed me. Although I struggled with it, I knew what must happen. His reach was long. But I'm a wife and a mother and a former victim. I had to be responsible for my actions. It tore my heart out to witness the abuse and the system, not giving a rat's ass about these women.

Surveillance began during my early morning walks, and whenever I was out in town alone, and decided that the only way to get to him was in the pre-dawn hours. Alan Stevens went to the gym every day. He parked his fancy car behind the gym and away from the rest of the patrons. His car was his prized possession, as each time he exited it, he walked around the car to check it, often buffing out smudges with his gym shirt. He wasn't as tall as Bart, but stockier and muscular, and I thought he'd be harder to take down.

The rain poured from the darkened skies, puddles formed on our lawn and in the street. I remember from my childhood, dancing in the puddles as the sun shined on me. The weather was like my mood. Dark. I knew what needed to happen but didn't want to do it after the rain. I planned to execute my target despite the weather. Low-hanging clouds and the misty drops were enough to cause havoc on the roads. Grateful for the inky cover of the early morning darkness, I left the house. Sometimes I believed the darkness matched my soul. Donovan's evilness has branded me. My scars were a testament to them. Each scar had a story, but never a reason to do what he did to me. Throughout the years, Jacob tried to erase those physical brands with his love and tenderness. He wasn't ever weak, he couldn't be. He was an officer of the law. But at home? He was all smiles, love and kindness. The mental scars, those are what push me, force me to take the law into my hands. To save my friends and protect the future. I headed to church and changed. I stepped into my too large running shoes I bought from the goodwill store. They were the only black pair they had; they looked like men's shoes. I added a thick innersole and tucked old socks in the toe. Once I tied them tight enough, I could run without worrying they'd hinder me, or I'd lose one. I watched from the building in the gym's rear, hiding behind an Arborvitae. I waited for Alan to park and walk around his car. This morning he parked next to the dumpster, the perfect place for a piece of trash like him. I slipped from behind the tree as he walked around his vehicle, rubbing the car with his shirt as he typically did. Wiping the vehicle of the marks only he saw. In his left hand was a small navy-blue barrel shaped bag. The same bag every day. I hit him as he stepped away from the vehicle. He stopped and froze as a wave of pain seized him, his knees buckling. The gym bag dropped, and it landed on his foot. He didn't feel the bag drop, nor did he smell the cologne from the broken bottle inside. His eyes closed; he tasted the blood that bubbled in his mouth. He felt the warmth as it poured onto his shirt. He tried to raise his hands to ward off another hit. I swung a second time, and his knees buckled. I dropped the note and ran. *Was it a tree branch?* His last thought as he collapsed onto the wet parking lot macadam. I turned mid run; he opened his eyes briefly as I slipped between the trees and waited. His last breath gurgled in his throat. I ran through the small section of trees that divided the property line. Passed my hiding spot and made my way back to the church office to change, with the weapon hidden in my oversized hoodie. The note I left said, **"Zeus, king of gods, the god of law, order, and justice. Justice is served!"**

THE OBSERVER'S HEART PANGS AS HE WATCHED ANDRESSA, TEARS streaming down her face as she hit the man. *Why is she doing this?* He followed the path she took when he heard the scream off in the distance.

Reaching for his phone, he pressed the number one on the keypad as he shoved his other hand through his thick, dark hair.

"Yes?"

"She killed another man. The same as the first."

"Stay on her." He cut the phone call off. The man known as

the observer was good at his job. He never got bored and suspected this would be an extremely interesting case. Eager for the day when he was told to capture her. He hurried to his home-based office, the small, older RV in the woods. It was easy to hide and a comfortable place to sleep while he watched his prey.

MICKIE ROGERS SLIPPED OUT OF THE SMALL BUNGALOW SHE shared with her husband and infant daughter. She headed two miles to her part-time job at Ace's gym. A small local gym owned by Ace Malone, a former boxer. She parked on the northeast side of the building, where the employees were told to park. They reserved the spots in the front for the members. She slipped inside and knew at once the night shift hadn't cleaned the gym. It smelled like a foot inside. The overflowing trash cans was her second clue. Cursing under her breath, she tossed her wallet into her locker and shoved the keys in the deep pocket of her leggings. She pulled open the utility closet and grabbed a huge clear trash bag. She emptied the men's room trash first, since there weren't any members inside yet. Then off to the ladies' room. When she made it to the gym. Beau, their newest trainer, arrived and helped. Micky unlocked the back door and pushed through and tossed the bag into the dumpster. Smells accosted her nostrils. Cologne, copious amounts and stale blood. As she neared the body, her focus was on her baby girl and the cold that kept them awake most of the night. When she left for work, Olivia was asleep on her father's chest. Shaking her head, she brought her mind back to her present tasks and tossed the second large trash bag, hoping it didn't explode, exposing the sanitary napkins. She glimpsed a thick leg covered in dark hair; she stepped forward and saw the body. "Mr. Stevens." Her voice came out in a whisper as she nudged his foot, praying he was not dead. "So much blood." At once, she came to her senses and screamed.

THE OBSERVER'S HEART SKIPPED A BEAT AS HE WATCHED THE GIRL because she was about to get the scare of her young life. Her face was pinched, and she sighed heavily as she carted the trash toward the dumpster. Her face changed suddenly, her mouth opened, she jerked her head back, and she moved her mouth. She covered her mouth when she saw the corpse. The observer can't hear or read her lips. Then came the terrified scream which summoned her co-worker. He fled the scene, taking the path that Andressa had.

BEAU HEARD MICKIE'S SCREAM. HE HURRIED OUT BACK AND found Mickie gagging; he stepped around her and saw the body; he stooped and placed his fingers on the man's wrist. "Call 9-1-1." He realized Mickie was in shock and took the phone from her and called himself. In a matter of minutes, the sirens blasted down rural route five.

Around nine thirty, the sheriff, Chuck, was on patrol when the call came in. Glancing at the bleak landscape, Chuck pulled to the back lot of the gym, where the deceased lay. Several minutes later, Jacob and Robert Gray, their newest rookie, arrived. Chuck took one look at the victim and called the Medical Examiner and then Rod. Bobby taped off the area and they waited while Chuck took the identification of the young woman who found him and the gym's trainer.

Rod Jackson was in the middle of his barbeque lunch when the call came in from the Clayton Heights Sheriff. They found another body behind a small local gym. The young gym attendant found him when she went to take out the trash. He was lying by the dumpster.

He sped down the highway, his car lights flashing. His gut told him the killer watched. He just had to figure out which spectator was guilty. He arrived at the secured scene, as the M.E. had pronounced the victim. A man in his 40s was lying on the ground with a severe head injury and bleeding. His gray-streaked hair matted with blood, while flies swarmed around the deadly wound. Rod took photos before stepping under the police tape, while he discreetly surveyed the gathered crowd.

"Who found the body?" he peered around, waiting for an answer. He fingered his gun while he perused the spectators. A nervous habit, almost as though he felt secure knowing his trusty weapon was by his side. Although trained in Krav Maga, he was also an expert shot and rarely missed his mark.

"She did." The young police offer pointed to a young woman, a stereotypical gym worker, tight abs, solid arms and fit tanned legs. Dressed in blue bike shorts, with a matching sports bra and a white racer backed tank top that read, "Ace's gym" on her breast pocket. Her dark hair was up in a messy bun and arms crossed as though she were cold. The officer passed Rod the info he had from her driver's license. She appeared to be in her twenties. Her face was tear-stained, and she trembled. Rod moved swiftly under the tape and toward her.

"Ma'am, are you okay?"

"No, I feel sick." She wrapped her arms around her stomach.

"Did you know him?"

"Not personally. He was a member, kept to himself. I work the morning shift because my husband works the second shift in San Antonio. He watches the baby so that I can work in the morning." Mickie rambled when nervous.

"Did you see him today?"

"No, he didn't come in. I found him when I took out the trash. The cleaning crew never showed last night, and the trash was overflowing." He glanced at the vacant warehouse, which sat behind the gym. Thick foliage blocked the view from the warehouse.

"Did either of you touch him?" Rod lifted his eyes toward her and the man who stood behind her, dressed in the same T-shirt.

"He did. He reached over to feel for a pulse, while I tried to call 9-1-1."

Rod looked up at the man behind. "And you are?" Rod asked.

"Names Beau. I'm the trainer on staff". He nervously pulled at his shirt.

"What do you recall?"

"I was in the back office. It's right there by the door, getting a training form, when I heard Mickie scream. I rushed out and saw Mr. Stevens. The blood pooled around his head. I leaned over to feel for a pulse and yelled for Mickie to call 9-1-1. She was shaking too much, so I grabbed her phone and made the call."

After interviewing the trainer, Rod walked around the building, looking for clues. Despite the crumbling concrete, there was nothing. He watched as litter blew past him onto the stretch of road. The slight breeze brought little relief to the scorching heat. He walked carefully over to the vacant warehouse, suspecting the killer had escaped through the trees. After spending a considerable amount of time he came up with just one footprint. He called the police officer over and asked him to secure it. Rod wouldn't head further into the trees in the event he'd overstep another print. The one he found was clear and indicative of a running shoe, from the size of it, a man's shoe.

He was relieved after calling the commissioner that an FBI profiler was on the way. He knew he was in over his head. Rod hung out at the bar after work; sometimes, it helped when he pretended to be inebriated and listened to conversations. He returned at ten that evening, dressed in jeans and a Cowboy's jersey, boots, ball cap, and wire-rimmed glasses that replaced his contacts. Rod took a bar stool, ordered a beer, and waited. He stayed until the bar closed at two in the morning. Annoyed because he heard nothing and still had to travel forty miles to his house. Bone tired and frustrated from almost pulling an all-nighter and for the lack of clues, except for the footprint. But it could be anyone's. He was told that often during nice days, some men who enjoyed running often ran into the woods for a better workout. It almost appeared the town was jubilant because of the murders. He climbed into bed, his mind and body weary, next to his sleeping wife. As he drifted off, he thought, *this guy will eventually fuck up, but until he does, we're all in over our heads.* Something had to give. Anything to help close this case.

Rod returned to Clayton Heights the following morning and heard that Georgia, the victim's wife, was awake and he headed for the hospital. He waited for what felt like hours. Even though she was awake, Georgia was confused and told Rod that her husband used to hit her frequently. He drove back to the Sheriff's office and saw Chuck coming from the break room out of his peripheral. "Chuck, lemme see that note again." Chuck nodded, and Rod followed him to his office. He placed the plastic bag holding the note on his desk, and Rod snapped a photo. His gut pinged that someone knew more than they were willing to divulge. He thought, *where are the leads? What am I missing here? Oh well, the FBI is on the way. They bludgeoned the attorney just as the drunk was.* Rod wrote himself a note, 'check for a connection–lawyer/client?' He asked the local cops to canvass again and drove back to San Antonio. He plopped into his desk chair and watched as the commissioner left the chief's office. He hurried over and knocked on the window, and after seeing the chief wave him in, he entered, shaking his head.

"Chief, the situation in Clayton Heights," he continued to shake his head.

"Pull up a chair, Rod, talk to me," Chief Owens replied.

"I'm not getting anywhere with the crimes over there. No one saw anything. The town despised the victims, and the Sheriff's office was short-staffed. They're in over their heads." For a few seconds, Rod wasn't confident that the chief was listening to a word he said.

"Do the best that you can and be on hand for the FBI. I left you in charge because you are a bulldog. Keep sniffing." The chief stood, signaling the end of the conversation. He hoped Rod was the one to solve the case. He hated looking like country bumpkins to the FBI.

Rod's red face radiated exasperation. "I spoke with the FBI and gave them what I had."

After months of investigations and interviews, Rod let the case rest, assuming the killer walked among the residents. Eventually, someone would slip up, and he'd get the lead.

The one thing the FBI agent told Rod was that killing is a rational choice, and it will not stop. Organized killers are highly intelligent and planners. But they eventually slip up. That was what Rod looked forward to, the slip-up.

Rod's brain was still processing the scene when he arrived at his desk. He worried about the lack of witnesses, no grieving spouses, no friends willing to discuss the deceased in a positive light. Almost as though they were gleeful.

Leaning over his desk, he turned on the outdated computer. While it went through the booting processes, Rod poured the thick black brew into his stained mug. He plopped down on the worn pleather seat and took a sip, and mumbled, "worst coffee ever."

Sixteen hours had passed since the last murder, bludgeoned behind the gym. *The reason? The only lead was revenge. But who? A client? His wife was still in the hospital, so it wasn't her. But who?* Rod tapped his pencil, organizing the thoughts in his head. While these deaths aren't senseless and tragic to the town's folks, they were still crimes and the killer was free to kill again.

Incoming calls were blowing up the police and the newspapers phone lines. The voices are always different, never filled with fear, almost amused.

Days later, they traced the phone calls to a young teenage boy with mental health issues. They brought him in for questioning and got a warrant to search his house. The only child of a single mother. She waited outside with the dog. As she waited for the search to end, she nervously twisted the dog's leash. The only thing they found was the voice mod the young man used.

Dozens of people were interviewed, and countless people gleefully admitted to the crimes. The mysterious deaths confound the police.

Eleven

After changing and cleaning the weapon, I had a good cry and flew up the basement steps and into the church to pray. A few other parishioners sat scattered in the pews, praying as well. I knew I'd probably go to hell for what I've done, but if it meant saving another life, I'd risk it.

Returning home, I noticed my mother-in-law had the babies out in their stroller. I saw them walking about ten houses down. I ran in and showered, sat on the shower floor, and cried. *Am I insane? I need to stop. It's destroying me inside, yet I can't let another woman suffer.*

I stood in the kitchen, my hair still dripping when they returned. My mother-in-law noticed my red eyes and asked if I was okay. I lied and told her I got shampoo in them and reached down to kiss my babies.

A few days later, Jacob told me the FBI was on their way and bringing in a profiler. I never gave my victims' names, just numbers. He was number three, the third to be committed to Hades because their wives lived in an earthly hell while they still breathed. Inmate number three sentenced to an eternity of shoveling turds in hell. I know I sound smug and cocky, but trust me, I'm not. I worry, I pray, but it is now my calling to end this suffering the only way I know how.

HE CLIMBED THE SMALL METAL STEP UP INTO THE MOTOR HOME. His home indefinitely. Wearily, he lowered the dinette table and covered the Formica top with cushions. He wrapped a white sheet over it and reached into the overhead cabinet for pillows. After a long day of following Andressa around town, he ate dinner and enjoyed a few tequila shots before crashing into his makeshift bed. His eyes shut as soon as his head hit the pillow. His dreams are of Andressa, the way her athletic body moves when she swings the weapon. He wakes up and wonders what it would be like to tap that. She isn't the first killer he's observed, but she is the first female. She is a challenge that made his job more interesting. All he needs to do is what the boss asked of him and to stay alive.

Andressa's motive is revenge. He understands revenge, more than most, when he avenged the rape of his wife. Yet he couldn't avenge her death. She couldn't cope with what had happened and ended her life. Leaving him alone. It's been a decade, and he still blames the rapist for his beloved's death.

Three days later, he followed his mark to the church. Worried that his sinful soul would combust if he went inside. Instead, he parked by a tree across the road and waited. Curiosity got the best of him and when he saw a church window crank open, he stealthily made his way to it and hovered low, listening to the meeting.

Twelve

R uby had the flu and asked me to host the meeting. Tonight's topic was, "Warning Signs." She had the notes prepared. I traded her a Tupperware container of chicken soup for her notes.

"Oh Andressa, you are a love. Thank you." She looked pale and was wearing a long flannel nightgown.

"I'll check in on you tomorrow. Thanks for the notes." I headed to church. The first half, the members spoke, shared stories. Then a brief break where we would enjoy pastries and hot beverages. I checked my watch, and it was time for a little education. I stepped to the podium and encouraged everyone to take their seats.

"As you are already aware, I'm filling in for Ruby, who is home with the flu. Please keep her in your prayers." I saw Pastor Robinson's encouraging grin. "Tonight, we're going to talk about warning signs." I gulped a mouthful of water and gazed toward the chairs.

"The relationship will move quickly. You may be engaged or married within months of meeting." I sipped from the water bottle. "They may say things like, 'You're all I need.' or 'I'd die without you.'"

"They feel threatened by your relationships with others and get jealous and accuse you of cheating. The abuser might even claim that being jealous is a sign of love. It isn't." I take a beat and let that sink in. It's classic. "They may follow you or ask friends to check in on you."

"Manipulation. They know your weaknesses. They prey on the vulnerable and use past pain to their advantage. They'll verbally abuse you to wear you down and make you feel it is your fault. They might withhold affection and try to control your money." There were murmurs, like "who cares?" I waited until the members settled down. "They may encourage you not to work with the promise that they will care for you. Some even use the threat of suicide. Mood swings are common. The simplest things can set them off or direct a cheerful mood into a pounding fist." Again, I wait while I see the nodding heads and hear the comments among them.

I begin again. "Often, they play the victim and will not take responsibility for their actions or poor choices. They are never at fault. Someone else is always to blame. They blame you. They may say they were drunk or high. Their vices or lack of self-control do not excuse their behavior."

"An abuser believes the world revolves around them. They are narcissistic. Women are beneath them or their husband isn't man enough. It is your job to meet his every need. You are his slave." A few members clapped, acknowledging the truth in this statement. "They are hypersensitive and see everything as a personal attack. They instigate fights, and blow things out of proportion, they're unpredictable."

"Your friends are stupid, slutty or you're cheating with them. Your family is too controlling, doesn't love you, or you depend too much on them. They put down everyone you know. Refuse to let you use the car or talk on the phone. Make it difficult for you to go to work. Try to cut off all your resources."

"You'll find yourself isolated or disconnected from family and friends, forcing you into submission and dependent on them. They're critical and no matter how hard you try to satisfy them or keep the peace and think nothing of verbally assaulting you or degrading you. They might promise to change. Or never yell or hit you again. Punish animals or children cruelly. Insensitive to pain and suffering. Tease children until they cry. Don't treat others with respect. Dismissive of others feelings. They might often shove, kick, or hit your animals out of anger."

"Some people talk about how their neighbor takes care of their pet or how their pet behaves when their partner is around." I continue, "They'll hurt your pets or destroy things that mean something to you as a way of hurting you. They are vindictive and use intimidation."

"Last, they have a history of violence. They might even have a police record for assault, fighting, or abuse. They believe that violence is a way to solve problems. When confronted, they claim someone provoked them." I folded the paper and peered around the room. "I later learned my abuser had beaten up an old girlfriend. The courts sealed his arrest record because he was only seventeen. His family paid her medical bills and offered a cash settlement."

"I probably know what you are thinking. It's too late, we are already in the situation. But now is the time to question yourself. Am I happy? Does my partner make me better? Am I confident around them? Do they support my goals? Why do we stay? Most for the paycheck. They have stripped us of everything, and we depend totally on our abuser. We stay because we're afraid to leave, knowing our abuse will worsen. The most important question is…" I wait a second for impact. "Am I safe?"

Thirteen

FBI Agent Benjamin Ellingson's flight landed early that morning. While the problems of the world were unimportant to him as only the murders were on his mind. He worked on the unsub's profile during the flight from Quantico. As he exited the airport, the Texas sky was clear, the sun bright as he picked up his rental vehicle. He opened the sunroof, allowing the sun to heat his head and neck. Rubbing the pain away, he observed his fellow travelers—anyone of them could be the killer.

Benjamin pulled into a spot in the Sheriff's department parking lot. He pulled open the back door and asked for the Sheriff.

Benjamin held out his hand. "Benjamin Ellingson."

Chuck gripped the proffered hand and gave it a vigorous shake. "Chuck Edwards." He squinted. "Ben, you look mighty young to be a profiler."

"It's Benjamin, and I am well trained. Don't let my appearance fool you." Internally seething because he hated being called anything other than Benjamin. "Has Adam arrived yet?"

"No, just you." He turned to the door to see who had arrived and pointed. "That's Jacob Swanson. He's a temporary detective now, and I assigned him to your team. His experience and life-long residency make him a valuable asset. He is valuable to your team. Chucked bellowed, "Jacob, come on over." After he introduced the two men, they hurried downstairs to the room where they would work. "It isn't much, but it's clean and well lit."

Jacob and Benjamin stood side by side and surveyed the room. An old conference table sat in the middle and a few white boards up front, along with two cork boards on stands. "It will do. My mobile is dead down here. We'll need to communicate by computer or old landlines."

"I can probably scrounge up some phones. Our equipment is old. I was told the FBI was sending in computers." Chuck nodded.

"They are. I'll double check on the communication devices." Benjamin dropped his briefcase and his luggage by the door. He walked around the room and rearranged it with Jacob's help.

Chuck nodded and left. "Jacob knows how to reach me if you need anything." Benjamin offered a dismissive nod and turned to Agent Rachel Foss.

"Foss, where can I find the files on each murder?"

"I organized them in the box on the ledge." She pointed. "Don't discount the fact the unsub could be a woman. Someone who could have been hurt or abused as well, resulting in mental damage. Probably from childhood."

Ignoring Agent Foss's opinion, he spoke. "Before we get to work, I want you to speak with the coroner." He pointed at Foss as he flipped through his notes. "Dr. Steven Butterworth? Is that the guy?" he cast his gaze at Jacob.

"Yeah, that's him." Jacob watched Foss reach for the keys and nodded as she left the room. As Foss headed across town, she spoke out loud to herself. "Don't gag, don't get sick." She's annoyed because she always gets shit jobs. The car approached the coroner's office at the edge of Clayton Heights, a mere block from the hospital. A one-story brick building with a glass double door in the center.

Foss stepped into the front office and pulled off her sunglasses. She reached into her back pocket for her credentials. She smiled at the receptionist as she passed her badge over. "I'm here to see Dr. Butterworth."

"Yes, Agent Foss. He is expecting you." She pointed to the double doors behind her and to the right. "I'll buzz you in." Once the door closed behind her, expecting crisp antiseptic smells, she crinkled her nose when whiffs of chemicals accost her senses. The area behind the reception room was a stark difference. Death lurked. Outside, life went on; across the road, doctors and nurses did their best to cure the ill and save lives. Beyond these doors, it reeked of death. Despite the smell of death here, outside was the beautiful lobby, cheerful with shiny marble floors dusted with flecks of gold. A small coffee cart sat just beyond the reception desk, the barista a petite older woman with a cheerful smile.

The agent's stomach rolled at the acrid scent of the deceased. No matter how many times she visited the morgue or was present during a postmortem, she never got used to the smell.

She knocked on the door and a physician dressed in green scrubs greeted her. After introducing herself, she asks, "What did you find?"

"Blunt force with something heavy."

"Any ideas of the weapon used?"

"Guestimate? A sledgehammer. It went clean through the skull to his brain. I found paint chips on his shirt, stuck to it with blood. Bone chips imbedded in his brain."

"Can you tell if the unsub was right or left-handed?"

"I'm sure that the person used both arms."

After viewing the body, Foss exited and removed the disposable scrubs. She strutted down the low-lit hallway further, adding to the macabre visit.

Foss arrived back at the station, finding that someone had drawn several red lines from the top to the bottom on the whiteboard. They numbered each block with the victim's name. Jacob read off the names to Benjamin as they finished their task. Afterward, Jacob taped the photos of the deceased above their name.

Closer to four, the other team members of the task force arrived. San Antonio Detective Rod Jackson and FBI agents Adam McMurtry joined Rachel Foss, Benjamin and Jacob. After the introduction, Benjamin said, "Okay everyone, go check into the Bed and Breakfast. We'll reconvene tomorrow at eight."

Fourteen

Parker's stepfather Earl resurfaced the day we celebrated Jake's first birthday. He was beside himself, trying to get into Parker's house. He'd disappeared years ago after neighbors found Parker's mother's body face down in the lake behind their house. She hated water and never went near the lake. Parker knew Earl did it. He threatened it enough, knowing her intense fear of water.

When Parker and Rosie were late for Jake's birthday party, I called Rosie. She had moved into Parker's house a few months ago. She said there had been an ugly scene, and Parker just flew out the door. Earl tried to get into the house, threatening both Parker and Rosie with a pry bar. He broke the window in the foyer and Parker told Rosie to come to us for safety. She was in the car on the way. Once she arrived, she told us about the altercation while Parker went to the hardware store to buy a replacement glass.

Parker showed up several hours later, after all the guests had left, smiling as though everything was okay in his world. Parker and Rosie announced their plans to marry. She was having a baby and wanted to marry him before the baby came. After we put our children to bed, the four of us hung out on the patio. I tried to get Parker alone, but it was impossible. While we sat planning their wedding, Jacob's phone went off. There was a break in at the grocery store, and they needed his help. Our small town was just so short-staffed, and although Jacob was off, they called him.

Earl continued to harass Parker and Rosie. Following Rosie to the grocery store, following her to the nursery school where she worked. Hoping to follow her inside the home and not leave. Parker got restraining orders, and he insisted the house was his as the surviving spouse of the deceased. Parker showed the will, which left the house to him, his mother's house, hers, and Parker's father before he died. Yet Earl continued to stalk them, one time making his way inside as Rosie brought groceries into the house. Earl threatened her and their unborn baby. He told her he'd toss her into the lake like he did his wife. She got a call through to 9-1-1, and they threw Earl into jail. Unfortunately, they didn't hear what he said about Parker's mother. He was in jail for two days and released. Parker and Rosie got the restraining order, but he still showed up whenever Parker was at work. They found Earl's body behind Parker's home, floating in the lake while they were in the hospital, awaiting their baby's birth. I had bludgeoned him. The note read, **Poseidon, the god of the sea, earthquakes, and storms, has delivered evil to the water's depth. Justice is served.**

HE WATCHED AS SHE SWUNG THE SLEDGEHAMMER, HITTING THE stocky older man on the side of his head. She got him in one quick stroke. Was it because he was weak, or was she that strong? He watched as she dipped the weapon in the lake before heading away on foot. Her face changed when she killed. Her jaw was tight, her eyes lifeless, her body rigid.

He'd report later. For now, he wanted to see what she planned next.

~

I'M TIRED OF THE HEAD PAIN AND AM RELYING ON MEDICATION increasingly to push through the intensity. I never had headaches before Donovan's abuse. He enjoyed zeroing in on my head at the onset, and I guess because it made me weaker, unable to fight back, dizzied me. The brutal punches always knocked me down so that he could kick me into the darkness. On colder, damper days, my body remembers every kick, punch, and injury. I use medication sparingly because I'm a mother and need to be there one hundred percent for my children and Jacob. I worry about my family, but I'm not foolish enough to believe I won't get caught. Does my need to keep my friends safe outweigh the fierce love I have for my family? NO! I do this for my family, for Alyssa, so nothing like this can ever happen to her.

Life went on peacefully for months. The frail older pastor remained at our declining church. He struggled with arthritis in his knees, ankles, and hips. I continued to help him, keeping the church clean and bringing him anything he needed from the basement. He often asked me to look things up on the internet for him. He trusted me, and my guilt was overwhelming.

If he expected a delivery, he'd call me to let me know it arrived. One time he got Jacob on the phone, he'd ordered a new printer and a case of paper from the local office supply store. I'd often print his information from the web, exercises to help with the pain. Home remedies, we'd often try the recipes together in the kitchen of the pastoral house.

I'd been out shopping with the kids, and when I returned, Jacob asked me why the office in the church basement was locked. Thankfully, I thought quickly and said, "There is cash inside that room, honey. I've been doing the books for Pastor Robinson and sometimes I leave the deposits inside until I can get the money to the bank." A partial truth, when in fact the money was kept in the safe in the upstairs office until I could get to the bank. I took a deep breath. "Did you need to get in?"

"Oh, no, babe. The office supply place delivered a case of paper and a new printer, and I figured I'd put it inside. It was heavy for you, but I realized Parker was still an active member, and he could lift it for you. I left it by the door."

I know what I did next was wrong, but I hated lying to the love of my life. I went over and kissed him passionately, knowing full well it would lead to lovemaking to refocus his brain on intimacy and making love and shut down his police brain.

Later, I opened another journal. I'm grabbing them at random now. The abuse journals. It's almost like I need to relive the horrors to justify my guilt.

January 1

Well, last night was fun. Not. We had to sleep at his parents' because Donovan's drinking was out of control. Thorton approached me and told me to get my husband in control. I snickered, and his eyebrows raised. I asked if Mrs. King could control him. It slipped out. I shouldn't have said it, as I'd already suspected he abused her. Donovan had to learn it somewhere, right? I tried to get Donovan into his bed upstairs. It was his mother who helped me. She had control. After the guests left, Shirley gave me a pair of pajamas and I joined Donovan in his bed. I must have overslept; the sun came up before I dozed off. While I slept, Thorton told Donovan of my remark. He berated me all the way home. Once at home, he backhanded me in the mouth, splitting my lip. I hate him.

Fifteen

The FBI set up a media conference outside of the police station. Many residents flocked to the station to watch in person. Not from fear, but curiosity.

Benjamin stepped to the podium. "I'm Benjamin Ellingson, FBI Profiler. We have little information on why or who is killing these men. There are no clues or witnesses."

"Serial killers come in all shapes, sizes and all genders and professions." He ran his fingers through his thick, dark hair. "Because everyone knew these men as abusers and even if there was a witness, there has been no thorough investigation. The killer is off the radar, but a mistake will happen. All we need is a sliver of DNA—hair, a drop of blood."

After answering the reporter's questions, a young man stepped up. "I'm Alan Stevens Junior. My dad was a victim of this serial killer."

"I'm aware of who you are. Your social media page is blowing up posts." The opinions on social media seem to be fifty/fifty. The men want the killer found, the women's opinion is to let it go, another abuser is gone. "Son, let us do our jobs. I feel your pain and assure you I will get this killer." Post after post from this young man, *someone killed my dad, someone had to see it.*

"Keep in mind, predators stay where they are comfortable, they are homegrown terrorists." Benjamin gazed at the spectators. "A murderer walks free among us. The FBI is taking over this investigation because the police's hands are tied. I'll say it again. A murderer walks among us. They could be here, watching or standing beside you right now. A monster." As expected, the residents gasped and turned toward one another.

He left and walked swiftly to the war room they'd set up in the basement. The equipment had arrived, and they were ready to dig in. Benjamin poured a cup of coffee from the brewer and stood. "You saw the papers? We're being made to look like idiots." Benjamin ran his fingers through his hair.

"The entire town saw the papers," Jacob curtly replied.

"Yeah, front page news. The headline in large letters, FBI BAFFLED!" Benjamin slammed his pen down. "They showed a picture of the victim, Stevens. He looks like an angel." He snorted and looked pointedly at Agent Foss. "The article also mentioned the FBI suspects a woman." Foss didn't squirm at his stare and her eyes never left his. Challenging.

Rachel murmured, "Well, at least someone agrees with me. Incidentally, I did not speak to the press."

Benjamin, unsure if he should believe her, inhaled and continued, moving to his orderly desk. He pulled the photo of the footprint found at the scene. He slammed it onto the board and shoved a pin through it. His vehemence shocked the team. Rachel snorted, unperturbed by his petulance. "This is what we know. We have an apex predator, meaning they are comfortable killing." He steepled his hands in front of his mouth. "Predators hunt prey. They stalk, learn habits. There is evil inherent in human nature." He sipped the coffee. "What do we know at this moment?"

Jacob answered, "The locations have zero footage. There are no security cameras."

"Yes, and that adds another layer of difficulty. What else?"

"It's been said that even if there was a witness, no one would come forth because they despised the victims."

Benjamin stepped away from the boards. "The killer is intelligent, maybe an average person. Like I said outside, could be someone who walks among us, who was there in the audience. The unsub went to college and hides their true self, the evil from those close to them. A successful criminal will do the same crime, the same way each time. This animal must be caught and caged. There is no cavalry coming, it's us." He waved his hands to the team. "The killer thinks they are normal, not crazy."

Rachel raised her hand. "Could it be a copycat killer?"

"No but do the research." Rachel felt dismissed. She knew she should speak; she was persuasive. After all, she became the master debater through college. She earned a lot of ribbing from other students after being called the master debater by her professor. Yet Benjamin ignored her as though she were unimpressive. He stood gazing at the whiteboard as if one victim would offer a clue.

Benjamin continued. Rachel concluded he liked the sound of his own voice, and his self-importance impressed him. So far, he has not impressed her. At all.

The small café in town delivered their lunch, and still, he didn't stop talking. As they ate their sandwiches, he continued. "These are revenge killings. Someone close to one victim. It's brutal, gory and not something a woman is capable of." He looked pointedly at Rachel. "We're looking at someone with upper body strength. The M.E. says all but one victim was hit once."

He stood at the whiteboards and grabbed a sandwich, taking a huge bite. Chewing noisily and swallowing huge gulps. Rachel thought her head was going to explode. She watched as Jacob stood and left the room. Rachel followed him, stopping by the beverage vending machine as Jacob dropped in his coins. He turned toward her. "Want one?"

"No thanks, I have water."

"What's up?"

"Jacob, every day we are in this conference room staring at the boards and the info we have on each victim. Timelines, their hangouts, habits. Every day we talk about them. We need to do more. All Agent Ellingson is interested in is hearing himself speak." A chuckle slipped from Jacob's mouth. "We've learned all there is about these crimes, the murders. We now need to hunt for the killer." She turned toward the door. "He thinks he's superior, and all knowledgeable about serial killers. Yet he refuses to even think the unsub could be female." She tucked a strand of dark hair behind her ear and smiled ruefully as she stepped to the coffee brewer and reached for one of Andressa's cookies. She thought she was ready for this. The investigation. Foss was ill prepared for how much misogyny would impede the investigation.

"Anger and revenge motives never give a good ending. We'll catch him." Jacob reached for one of his wife's cookies. He never talked about dissatisfaction with his job. He was a good guy, one that took pride in his work. Yet not being able to find what the press is dubbing the Mythology Killings weighed heavily on his mind, as did the team. The townspeople didn't grieve the deaths, they were almost joyful. The victims were "Pieces of shit," "pond scum," and "heartless abusers." Internally, he agreed, but people cannot take justice into their own hands. *Could this be a group? Vigilantes?*

Later that afternoon, Jacob and Benjamin parked behind the gym and sat quietly. There was little light back there, just one yellow bulb. In the early morning and late at night, it would be very dark. If the killer wore dark clothing, he wouldn't be seen. "There's not a lot of cover here. The unsub exited through the warehouse parking lot and through those trees, where we found the footprint. We're still waiting on type and size."

"Why are we back here, Benjamin? Do you suspect he's after someone else?"

"No. I suspect that whoever did this has great upper body strength, and this is the only gym in town." He focused on the back door, and no one used it. "Jacob, if you were the killer. What would you have done?"

"Assuming I don't go to the gym?"

"Yes, that works."

"I'm not sure, because I don't have a criminal mind. But assuming a person was in trouble, and if it were me, not the police, but an average citizen, I'd probably hide somewhere. Maybe behind one of those thick trees. Except I'm wider than the trees that line the warehouse." He squinted toward the old vacant building. "The warehouse. Maybe that's his home base, or he broke in to hide and watch."

"Let's go, Jacob." The men pulled their service weapons and searched the building, finding a window opened in the rear. Benjamin's intuition assured him he'd find something here. A smidgen of a clue would validate him.

As the bright sun lowered, the milky moon appeared. The air had a coolness that evening. Benjamin, with the warrant in his pocket, headed to the sleepy neighborhood. He waited until Jacob left for the day. He observed the houses, each distinct, lawns cut to perfection showing pride of ownership. An occasional basketball hoop on top of the garage. Suburbia at its finest. Benjamin was almost gleeful that he would disrupt this quiet neighborhood with the arrest. He knew who the Mythology Killer was, despite the close relations with the officer working on the case. Benjamin knew, and now it was time to pay the piper. When he pulled up and parked next to the curb, he found a young girl in the driveway playing basketball, her curls bouncing as she tried to make the hoop mounted on the top of the garage door. She stepped inside when she heard the dinner call through the screen door. Benjamin stepped out of the rental, straightened the crease in his pants, adjusted his tie and slipped on his suit jacket. He walked to the front door and rang the doorbell, thankful that it wasn't one of the popular ones with a camera. Inside he heard a female voice say, "I'll get it, daddy."

The door opened and Benjamin asked, "Are your parents' home?"

"Yes. My mom is cooking dinner and dad is helping."

Parker recognized the voice and the agent. "Agent Ellingson, What's up?"

"Parker McCully, you are under arrest for murder. You have the right to remain silent. Anything you say can be used against you in court. You have the right to talk to a lawyer for advice before we ask you any questions. You have the right to have a lawyer with you during questioning."

The little girl started crying, and Rosie ran to the front door. "What's going on? Dinner is ready."

"Honey, there's been a mistake. Can you call Jacob and get me a referral for a lawyer? He should know all the good ones." Rosie leaned over and kissed him as tears streaked down her face.

"I'm on it." Rosie tossed a sidelong gaze to the FBI agent.

Officers arrive from San Antonio with a search warrant. Rod was among them. *Finally, a break in the case.* The family left the house and Rosie had the kids eat their dinner at the picnic table on the patio. An hour later, Benjamin came outside with a bag, carrying an old metal baseball bat that had seen better days. Its handle was red and appeared to match the chip found on one of the deceased.

The police processed Parker, fingerprinted him, had him strip and change into a tan police issued jumpsuit. They offered Parker a defense attorney, but later learned that Jacob called in a favor with a criminal attorney friend.

Within hours, the forty-year-old attorney, known as the bulldog, strode through the police station doors and to the desk, and demanded to see his client, Parker McCully. The young officer as the desk cockily asked, "Who might you be?"

"I'm Jarrod J. Snyder, counsel for Mr. McCully. The officer sneered and pressed the button on his phone angrily. Another officer appeared and escorted the attorney to the interview room. The officer shoved Parker into a chair and attached his handcuffs to a metal loop on the table's top. Shaking his head, the attorney spewed, "Privacy, please, while I confer with my client." After the officer left, the attorney pulled up a chair, flipped open his briefcase, and pulled out a leather-bound folder with a yellow legal pad inside. He clicked open a gold pen and jotted down the date, time, and Parker's full name at the top of the page. "Mr. McCully, may I call you Parker?"

"Yes, Mr. Snyder."

"It's Jarrod. Parker, these are some serious charges. I haven't had a chance to go over the evidence yet. But I will. Unfortunately, they won't release you on bail. Tell me in your own words what happened this evening."

Parker articulated what transpired after he returned home from work.

"We've got a tough case, Parker. But I'm prepared to fight for your innocence."

"Jarrod, I didn't kill anyone. You've got to believe me." Parker's eyes stung.

"I believe you, so does Jacob. That's why I'm here. We'll need to form a timeline of where you were during each murder. I'll also need character witnesses." They conferred for another hour when Jarrod agreed to return in the morning.

THE OBSERVER LEARNED OF THE ARREST IN THE MORNING EDITION of the Clayton Heights newspaper. He reached for his cell phone and called the line that only his boss would answer.

"What's wrong?"

"They have arrested a resident for the crimes."

"So?"

"He's innocent!"

"Your job is to keep me informed, not to be judge and jury." A long, drawn-out sigh escaped. "What we do isn't morally gray, it's much darker. We are criminals ourselves. Just stay on her. I want an immediate update on anything she does. Do you understand?"

"Yes sir, I understand."

A snigger burst through the phone. "If your conscience is bothering you, I'll send someone else."

While his boss hit the nail on the head, he knew he'd probably end up in the sea if he asked to be taken off the job. "I'm fine, I've got it covered, boss."

Without a word, the call disconnected.

He kept inconspicuous by changing his appearance. Since his appearance was average, without defining characteristics, he could blend in with the locals easily. He often changed his appearance, grew a beard, shaved his head, grew his hair out not to be recognized as a stranger in town. He looked like more than one stranger.

THE FBI MOVED QUICKLY AND IN A MATTER OF DAYS, THEY transferred Parker to the jail in San Antonio. The Clayton Heights police worried neighbors would try to break Parker out of their small local jail. Protestors, mostly females, stood outside the jail, day in and day out. The town's women didn't give a hoot, and many of the male population had voiced their concerns.

Days later, Parker entered the courtroom in chains, pale and thin. His hand shook. He wasn't used to living like this and it overwhelmed him from being away from his wife and girls.

"All rise. The circuit court of San Antonio is now in session. The honorable Judge Alfred Hankins presiding," the bailiff bellowed. "You may be seated."

"Mr. McCully, you are charged with four counts of murder in the first degree. How do you plead?" the Judge asked, almost bored.

Parker stood, his entire body visibly shaking, "Not guilty, Your Honor."

The Judge nodded toward the court stenographer, a woman in her sixties, her fingers, despite being crippled with arthritis, typed furiously.

"Is the state ready?" asked the judge.

"Yes, we are, Your Honor," the district attorney, Wilson Goodall, replied.

"Is the defense ready to present its case?"

"No, we are not, Your Honor."

"Why?" the Judge asked.

"Your Honor, my client hired me three days ago, and it's been a challenge to get the Clayton Heights P.D. to give us the incriminating evidence."

"I'll grant the request for a continuance, but I warn you Mr. Snyder, this is the only delay I'll permit."

For weeks, Jarrod's assistant, Donna Kellerman, spent time in Clayton Heights to gather intel on Parker and the townspeople's opinion. Not one resident thought Parker was guilty. No one had an opinion on who was.

Suddenly Clayton Heights became a tourist trap. The residents were eager to engage in gossip with anyone that would listen, even strangers.

A week later, Judge Hankins called the courtroom to order. This would be to choose the jury. None of whom came from Clayton Heights. All morning long, the attorneys asked questions of the prospective jurors. Jarrod knew which ones he would go to bat for. By dinner hour, they selected twelve jurors after going back and forth between the lawyers.

"We'll call it a day. Court will resume at eight tomorrow morning. Bailiff, dismiss the jurors. The judge cast his gaze toward the jury box. "I remind you not to discuss this case among yourselves or with anyone else."

The following morning, dawned with cloudy skies, Jarrod was surprised to find that a crowd had already gathered on the courtyard steps. The press and curiosity seekers. Judge Hankins settled himself behind the bench and asked for opening statements.

The prosecutor stepped forward. "Thank you, Your Honor. The state will prove that the defendant, Parker McCully, is guilty of the murders that took place in Clayton Heights over the last decade. We prove that Mr. McCully is, in fact, the Mythology Killer. We will prove motive, means and opportunity."

"Mr. Snyder, you may now make an opening statement."

"Thank you, Your Honor." Jarrod turned toward the jury, buttoning his suit jacket. "Ladies and Gentlemen of the jury. The Mythology Killer is real. The perp has killed four people. That's a fact. We can't dispute that. What is disputable is who did it. What would Mr. McCully's motive be? The defense will show credible witnesses that Mr. McCully was otherwise engaged during most, if not all, the murders. Once while his wife gave birth at the hospital." Someone in the back gasped. "Is Parker McCully the serial killer? That's what you'll have to decide. Unless the prosecution can prove he is, without a doubt, then you must acquit. It is your responsibility to uphold your duty as a juror in this case." Jarrod turned toward the bench. "Thank you, Your Honor."

The bailiff swore in the first witness. The mouth of the south, as he became known to the local media, the son, Alan Stevens, Jr. who has been blasting his father's murder all over social media, snorted when they called Rod Jackson to the stand.

Rod walked, his gait almost reflected his exhaustion, his wife had a health scare, and the visits to the hospital drained him, as did his worry for his wife. He placed his hand on the Bible at the bailiff's request, "Do you solemnly swear or affirm to tell the truth and nothing but the truth, so help you God?"

"I do," Rod answered, knowing that was the only answer expected. Rod plopped into the hard wooden seat.

"Detective, do you recognize exhibit A?"

"Yes, it's the baseball bat we retrieved from the defendant's house."

"Can you tell me how it was found?"

"A search warrant was obtained by the FBI lead. He found it hidden in the garage."

"Objection. The bat wasn't hidden, it was visible, among all the other baseball equipment. My client is a baseball coach."

"Sustained." The judge nodded to Mr. Jackson, "Go on."

"I didn't find the bat. I was told where they found it."

The prosecutor cast his eyes to his assistant. "Told by whom?"

"Agent Ellingson, the lead FBI agent on the case." He nodded his head toward Benjamin.

The prosecutor was furious. He felt deceived by the slick FBI agent. "Thank you, Detective." He turned and walked toward his assistant, knowing the first crack in his prosecution appeared with the very first witness.

The judge eyed the defense. "Mr. Snyder, you may cross-examine."

Buttoning his suit jacket as he stood, an arrogant smile on his face, he said, "Thank you, your Honor." He approached the bench, his gaze on the pink-faced detective. "Detective, did you see the weapon, the baseball bat, up close?"

"Yes, sir. I did."

He slammed a photo down in front of him and walked to the jury and passed them and enlarged photo of the bat found in Parker's garage. He passed another photo of the paint chips found embedded in the victim's wound. "Mr. Jackson, this bat has a red handle, with wear marks, but I wouldn't say the paint has chipped."

"Sir, I can't answer to that, as I am not an expert, but I can see where you would draw that conclusion."

"Thank you, Detective Jackson." Jarrod turned toward the Judge; confident he started the mistrial. He knew and believed wholeheartedly that his client was being set up by an over-eager FBI agent who was full of himself.

The agent in question was called to the stand next. After the prosecutor had his turn, Jarrod stepped up and was ready to swipe the floor with him. Known for being vicious in the courtroom, he came out hard.

"Exhibit B shows two colored paint chips taken from the skull of Alan Stevens. A red fragment and a yellow. As you can see in exhibit A, the handle of the bat shows wear but not chips. What doesn't show is yellow. They found the other fragments in the victim's skull. In my humble opinion, this bat cannot be the weapon used to commit these crimes."

They heard gasps from the audience. "Order." The judge issued an order to the jury to suppress all audible emotions. Tears sprung to Rosie McCully's eyes as her palm flew to her mouth, covering the gaping circle it made. She prayed that this would be the first step in declaring the mistrial Jarrod spoke to her about. Jarrod's no-nonsense approach to defending her husband offered her hope. She was also very thankful to Jacob for introducing them to Jarrod.

As Jarrod walked back to his client, he winked at Rosie, who beamed at him.

Three days later they declared a mistrial, and Benjamin Ellington high tailed it out of Texas.

Sixteen

Neither wealthy nor poor, Rachel Foss grew up in a middle class neighborhood. Her mother was a housewife, her father a salesman for a medical equipment company. He traveled a lot and he came home often angry and bitter. Rachel later learned he got her mother pregnant, and her parents forced him to marry her. Built on resentment, their marriage didn't stand a chance. Her father's resentment, her mother tried.

As technology changed, it was up to Rachel to educate him. Those were the only times he called home when he had issues with his phone, laptop, or spreadsheets. He never thanked her, just said, "Gotta go, I'm busy." He was the classic narcissist, and they were happiest when he was on the road.

The family lived in a brick two story home in a small community near Maryland's coast.

Rachel pulled the tab on a can of soda; she almost snickered out loud. *Old Daddio would shit a brick if he saw me drinking this.* He forbade sugary drinks and claimed they rotted teeth. They probably did with the amount of sweetener in them. In reality, it was because he didn't want to pay dental bills.

She plopped into her chair next to Jacob. She could tell his frustration by the way he pounded on the keys. Normally a quiet man, with a scowl on his usually pleasant face, was a clue, too. He caught her looking at him and she asked, "Are you alright?"

"Yeah, just frustrated. We can't seem to catch this guy. All we know is he is clever." He eyed McMurtry who stepped in for Ellington. "I don't think the perp lives here. I know most of these people. I have my whole life." Sighing, he stood. "Humans are messy and complicated. I'm embarrassed to admit we are in way over our heads."

Nodding, Foss slid her chair back and stood. Her loafers tapped on the concrete floor as she reached for the small backpack, she placed by the coat rack. She reached inside and grabbed a protein bar. She ate one every morning at ten. Seeing Jacob's eyes on her, she asks, "Want one?"

"No thanks. Andi prepared a huge breakfast this morning." He tapped his flat stomach. "I'm stuffed."

"She cooks you breakfast?"

"Yep. Every workday. Packs my lunch too. She is the best part of my world." Jacob gulped from his stainless steel water bottle. "I know this sounds far out there, but do you think someone hired this killer?"

"Good theory, but no. I think whoever is right under our noses." She tossed the wrapper into the trash can. "I can think of only one family who could afford to do it. The Stevens'. I mean, he paid for sex. Which was covered up after they caught him. His wife came from old money, but she's not all there and he's dead, so we'll never know." She shrugged her shoulders. "We'd be up against who exactly. Their kid?"

"I'm stumped. What do we do? Rachel, I can't voice my thoughts to these guys, they're so full of themselves."

"I get it. I feel the same. So, what's the next step?"

"The party at church. They have invited you?"

"Yeah. I saw your wife at the grocery store. Andressa told me about it and said I was welcome."

"Let's hang out and listen. Observe the attendees."

Foss nodded and turned to her laptop and continued with her tasks.

Seventeen

The guilt consumed me, not because I committed the crimes they charged Parker with, but for Parker suffering the consequences of my actions. I. Must. Stop. I was confident that I would. After all, I am not insane. Right? Or am I? Did all the hits to my head alter my reality and I'm unaware? After dropping the kids off at school, I hurried to the park for a run. I preferred the high school track, but never used it while school was in session; only on the weekends, if there wasn't a game. Running cleared my mind. After stretching I sprint off, my breath even. Halfway around, I feel the telltale burn kick in. I went over in my mind how I've taken out the town's trash. I then focus on my escape plan should someone realize it's been me all along. Parker was a dear friend, and its why Jacob got him the best criminal attorney out there. Jarrod Snyder had a reputation and more acquittals than any other criminal attorney in the area. His hourly rate was high, but after speaking with Jacob, he offered to take on Parker's case pro-bono. No one in our town had the money for this highly intelligent attorney from the city. If he wasn't free, we would be willing to host a fundraiser for our dear friend.

On the Sunday after Parker's release, I started an enormous party for Parker and family after services. It thrilled pastor Robinson to host, and I did most of the cooking in the church kitchen with our beloved pastor tasting each dish. The neighbors promised to bring a covered dish and almost the entire town showed up, except for Alan Stevens Junior. He wanted the criminal caught and even if it wasn't Parker; he wanted someone behind bars. His social media was still blowing up with posts, yet it seemed his followers were commenting less and less. The party began at noon and lasted until ten o'clock. Jacob took a vacation day and at some point, the entire police and fire department visited for a bite to eat. People came and went with fresher food being supplied throughout the day. The small bar in town donated trays of buffalo wings. Parker felt our love, but the guilt was all-consuming for me. The FBI arrested our closest friend because of the things I did. I struggled.

Jacob pulled me into his embrace as we watched the fireworks that the fire department put on. "Are you okay, sweetheart? You seem off."

"Yeah, I'm good. Just thinking how horrible this could have gone if they sent Parker to prison for a crime he didn't commit."

"The truth always comes out, don't worry. We'll find the killer."

I pressed my lips to his as though I agreed. They would eventually find out it was me. I'm not stupid enough to believe I won't make a mistake. I promised myself to put the journals away or burn them, not to relive those horrible times and to put them behind me.

The fireworks display was beautiful. Parker had his arms wrapped around his wife as their girls laid on a bright pink blanket on the grass, watching the beautiful display in the sky.

Our children watched from a picnic table with their grandmother. I loved this small town, but still I needed to stop. It's not my place to protect it. I will stop, I promised myself. I will throw away the journals.

Eighteen

Our lives resumed normally for some time. We still had our support group, but very few new members. We worried if it was because of the women's fears or did the abusers behave because of the connection the deaths held? The FBI left after months of investigations.

The migraines I suffered intensified in duration and frequency. I didn't complain to Jacob and pushed through. Although we tried to have another baby, it just never happened. We were happy and still so in love. Jacob never brought sadness into our home, no matter what horrors he saw as a police officer. That was one reason I didn't complain about migraines.

We took our family on another vacation, this time on a cruise. Just like the one we took on our honeymoon. The kids enjoyed island hopping. Jacob saved our tax refund for this trip. Glory enjoyed it, too. I loved having her with us, and it thrilled Jacob to do this for his mother. Jacob rented jet skis, and he and the kids went on an adventure on them. It was the highlight of their trip. Glory and I stayed behind on the ship and went to the spa, as part of our Mother's Day gifts from Jacob and the children. It embarrassed me during the massage that my scars were visible. When Glory gasped and asked me what each one was. "Mom, I don't think I should tell you."

"I want to know. I'd like to kill the man that hurt you."

I almost said, "Too late, I already did." Instead, I replied, "He's dead. He overdosed."

"Talk to me, sweetheart. Does it help to talk?"

"It did, but now I try to forget."

"Well, those scars are a reminder of the battle you won. I hope he's rotting in hell."

"Yeah, me too." *But I'll probably rot in hell next to him for what I've done.*

"Don't let the scars embarrass you. Let's enjoy the massage and the mud bath. I shouldn't have questioned you."

"Mom, you can ask me anything. Any time! It was just horrible, and I don't want to taint this amazing vacation. Are you having fun?"

"Oh, my Andi, I feel like the rich and famous. We're about to take a mud bath. Never in my wildest dreams did I think I would ever get a massage, much less a mud bath." She giggled.

Glory and I were next to each other in the mud baths. I climbed into the cool mud and sat down and watched one attendant assist Glory. They scented the room with essential oils. When Glory plopped into the tub, the mud squished, and Glory couldn't stop giggling. "Tell me about this mud."

"Its mineral water mixed with mineral rich clay."

"What do these baths help with?"

"The brochure said they draw out impurities, exfoliate dead skin."

"Well, I got a lot of that, since I got one foot in the grave and the other on a banana peel." Glory snickered. "What else?"

Laughing, I said, "They relax sore muscles and joints. Improve the skin and relieve arthritis pain."

"Oh maybe I'll feel so wonderful. I'll dance at the fancy cocktail party tonight."

"I'd love to see that, Mom. Maybe we'll find an agreeable gentleman to dance with you."

"My handsome grandson promised me a dance."

SHORTLY AFTER OUR CRUISE, ALYSSA ASKED IF ONE OF HER closest friends, Jasmine, could stay the week while her mother went to Alabama to care for her ill mother. Of course, I said yes. Two adorable fourteen-year-olds giggling would make me happy. They met on the first day of kindergarten and have been close ever since. Jasmine was a lovely girl, quiet and mannerly. I noticed at once how haunted her eyes were. She seemed fearful of Jacob when she hadn't been before. Jacob, the gentlest person I'd ever met, as well as our son, Jake. He was two years younger than the girls but grew tall and lifted weights in school. He was also on the wrestling team. Although he looked like his father, he was tall, like my brothers. I didn't hear the expected giggling. Jasmine was serious and guarded. Alyssa was respectful of whatever Jasmine was feeling. They didn't use the pool, except for sitting on the edge with their feet dipping. From what I could see, they didn't speak. My eyes welled with tears when I saw Alyssa reach for Jasmine's hand and give it a good squeeze. Prideful of the sweet and kind daughter I'm raising, I smiled.

A few days after Jasmine's arrival, the girls wanted to bake cookies. After checking for flour and not finding any, I reached for my purse to head to the grocery store to get flour and some fun decorations when Jasmine asked if she could come with me. Alyssa stayed home with her brother and grandmother. My poor mother-in-law was slowing down and struggled to walk most days. After being misdiagnosed for many years, the new rheumatologist ordered tests and found she was suffering from Multiple Sclerosis. Still, she insisted on being productive somehow. I didn't need her to do anything for us but enjoy her golden years, and I didn't intervene and let her do as she wished.

My heart broke for the teenager, whose hands shook consistently. It concerned me. "Jasmine, have you ever been to Parking Latte?"

"No, ma'am. My stepfather would get madder than a mule chewing on bumblebees if he knew we spent money on fancy drinks."

Smiling at Jasmine's analogy, I watched her nervously, biting her lower lip. I pulled into the parking lot and said, "Let's have a snack and something decadent to drink." I smiled.

Jasmine returned the smile, tentative, and slid out of the passenger seat. Her oversized jeans were clinging to the back of her legs on a sweltering day. After we decided what she would like to try, we picked up our order and sat at a table for two in the back, under a canopy next to the colorful coffee truck. Jasmine sipped her cold beverage and said, "Thank you so much, Mrs. Swanson, this is yummy."

"You're welcome, sweetheart." I smiled. "Aren't you hot in those jeans? They're so heavy."

"No, I prefer to wear these baggy clothes. Makes my momma angry because she buys me nice girly things."

"Don't you like girly things?" Her previous feminine style sparked my curiosity. Often the girls dressed alike.

"I do, I love them! But this is better. I look like a boy."

Her answer surprised me, and I asked, "Well, you can look like, however, and wear whatever you want. But sweetheart, you are a beautiful young girl whether you're dressed like this or in girly things." I watched as her face changed expression, and tears pooled in her eyes. The struggle to control her emotions was obvious. I reached for her hand and held it, rubbing my thumb across the top of her hand to comfort her. The tears streamed down her face, and I heard a quiet sob. I got up from my chair and squatted next to Jasmine, pulling her into my embrace. "Sweetheart, if anything is bothering you, please share it with me. Mr. Swanson and I will protect you. I promise you!"

Jasmine sobbed quietly for a few minutes. She lifted her tear-stained face and whispered, "He touches me. He hurts me!"

"Who sweetheart?"

"My stepfather."

"Are you able to share what he does, where he touches you?" I asked.

The tears began again. "He comes into my bedroom on the nights my mom works late," Jasmine sobbed.

"Sweetheart, I promise to protect you. But you must tell me everything."

"You will? Can I live in your house? Away from him?"

"If your mother says it's okay, you're welcome anytime. Have you told your mother that he touches you?"

"I tried. She said he's just affectionate. But what he does? Only married people do!" Jasmine sobbed.

Honestly, she shocked and appalled me with her responses. I gasped audibly and tried to remain nonplussed. How did I know what she thought married people did? Did he penetrate this poor child? I held both of Jasmine's hands and said, "What do married people do, honey?"

"They have sex. We learned about it in school last year."

"Are you saying he forced you to have sex?"

"Yes, he puts his private part in mine, and it hurts so bad."

"Does Alyssa know?" I asked.

"Yes, she told me to tell you that you'll make it stop. She said you help a lot of women. Will you help me? Will you make him stop?"

"Yes, sweetheart, but that means I must speak to your mom. Is that okay?"

Jasmine lowered her head and whispered, "Yes," barely audible.

"Do you want to go back to my house now or to the supermarket?"

"Your house, you have flour. Alyssa hid it, so you'd go to the supermarket. We planned that I'd ask to go with you, so we could be alone and talk." Jasmine admitted with a sob.

I pulled Jasmine into my arms and hugged her tightly, whispering, "You brave girl, I've got you, honey, I'll take care of this, sweetheart."

"Promise?

"Cross my heart."

"Thank you. I don't want to have a baby. Can he do that, put a baby in my belly?"

I nodded and asked, "Are you late, honey? Do you think you can be?"

My heart dropped when she nodded. "Six weeks!" We stopped at the pharmacy, and I bought a pregnancy test. I had her take it to the restroom. When I saw the plus sign and looked at Jasmine, petite, and so young, she still wore pre-teen clothing. Bile rose in my throat, and I felt like I could murder the son of a bitch in broad daylight. I wrapped the positive test, shoved it in my purse, and hugged Jasmine. "I'll make this better, I promise you, and until he's out of the house, you are not going home!"

Jasmine sobbed the entire drive to my home. Alyssa waited anxiously on the front porch. "Alyssa, take Jasmine to your room. Watch TV or something. I need to speak to your father."

"Okay, mommy," Alyssa reached over and hugged me tightly, "I love you!"

"I love you too, sweet girl. Now take care of Jasmine. She'll be staying with us for a while. Please don't answer the front door without my knowledge. I need to speak to your father." With robotic motions, I peered into the family room, looking for Jacob. Jake was asleep on the sofa, and Glory watched her soap opera in the recliner. "Mom, where's Jacob?"

"In the garage, love," Glory looked up at me and said, "Are you okay? Do you have a migraine? You're pale, like a ghost!"

"I do. I'm okay, but I need to speak with Jacob," I replied, rushing into the garage. Jacob looked up when he heard the door open. I ran into his arms and sobbed. He caressed me and waited until I could speak. I looked into his eyes, and worry lines furrowed his forehead. "I need your help with something."

"Sit, babe!" He pulled out the stool from under his work-bench. He had his guns laid out and had been cleaning them.

I told him the entire story that Jasmine had relayed to me earlier. "Honey, child protective services need to be contacted. She'll have to be examined at the hospital." Jacob said.

"I promised to keep her safe, and now they'll place her in foster care."

"She will be safe, and we'll apply to foster Jasmine. We'll make it work, but we must get her examined. Get her something to eat while I shower. I'll be ready in fifteen minutes." Jacob said as he assembled his work revolver, his lips a grim line and his face stone-like. An expression I've never seen before.

I knocked on Alyssa's door and said to Jasmine, "Sweetheart, Mr. Swanson wants to take you to the hospital. Can you get your sneakers on?"

She nodded, crying again. She said, "Will you come with me, Alyssa too?" I nodded, fighting tears. "I'm making you girls a sandwich. Try to eat. It could be a lengthy process." I went into the kitchen, made the girls a sandwich, and popped two over-the-counter pain relievers.

Jacob stepped into the kitchen, dressed for work, looking as angry as before. He hugged me and said, "You're the kindest person I know. Together, we'll get this kid through this."

I nodded, knowing what I needed to do. But I was trying to follow the process, hoping it didn't fail this child as it had failed so many others. In the car, on the way to the hospital, I sent a text to Parker.

Me: I have a situation and need you to take over tonight's group meeting. Please?

Parker: What's wrong?

Me: Alyssa's friend Jasmine. You've met her many times.

Parker: Yes, the girls helped Tonya with her cheerleading routine to try out for the team. I know Jasmine, a genuinely friendly kid. What's happening?

Me: Her stepfather sexually abuses her!

Parker: How? Touching or all the way?

Me: The worst! A positive pregnancy test.

Parker: What do you need?

Me: Stand by...we're on the way to the hospital now. Jacob is with me. It could get ugly; the guy is a piece of work. We may need to get her an attorney of her own. I don't know her mother that well and am not sure of the reaction.

Parker: I will wait until I hear from you.

At the hospital, the doctor called Jasmine's mother for permission to be treated. After the examination and the police interview, child services released Jasmine to us at her mother's request. When contacted, she agreed we were the safest placement for her daughter.

The police picked up Lyle Dillard and took him to the county jail. When he saw Jacob and me, he yelled. "I didn't knock that girl up, their boy did! That's right, the cop's kid did it!"

I lunged for him, and Jacob pulled me back by my shirt. "Babe! Stop!"

I texted Parker.

Me: They picked up Lyle. When he saw Jacob and me. He blamed my baby boy! He accused Jake. My little boy! I knew that Jake and Parker were close. Parker took him on many camping trips. He was like a son to Parker since they'd had three daughters.

Parker: Heading to get Jake now. He trusts me, and I'll feel

him out. I'll be with him should the police come for questioning.

Me: Thank you, Parker, you're a good friend.

When Jasmine heard the accusations, she screamed, "Mrs. Swanson, it wasn't Jake, he's a little kid! The only thing he did to me was to steal my ball cap off my head, and that was a joke. He gave it right back. You know, he was that goofy, annoying little brother." Jasmine sobbed.

Parker confirmed what Jasmine said. Jake told him he'd never kissed a girl. And told his father the same thing. Jasmine stayed with us for two weeks when she stood by the kitchen sink, helping Alyssa with the dinner dishes. She bent over and wrapped her arms around her mid-section, moaning.

"Are you alright, sweetheart?" I asked.

"I … I'm not sure. Oh… Mrs. Swanson, it hurts bad." Jasmine darted into the powder room. Both Alyssa and I followed.

Alyssa knocked on the door. "Jazz, are you okay?" she asked.

"I think I just got my period!" Jasmine exclaimed. "But it hurts."

"Can mom and I come in?" Alyssa asked.

We heard the click as the door unlocked, and Jasmine stood, her pants pulled up. I peered into the toilet and saw what appeared to be a clump of flesh-colored tissue and a lot of blood. Just as I was about to say, don't flush. Jasmine flushed. I was hoping to get evidence for DNA. I wasn't even sure if they could capture DNA, but I wanted to try. We took Jasmine to the emergency room, where they sent her to the operating room and performed a dilation and evacuation curettage to retrieve the remaining tissue. God took care of her, and I was relieved, as was her mother. She was way too young for any of this.

They released Lyle Dillard on bail, waiting for his hearing. Jasmine remained with us until he was behind bars. After the trial, they released Lyle because school students incriminated my son. They said they overheard him brag about being intimate with Jasmine. Funny, though, none of the boys were friends with my son or on the wrestling team with him. I knew exactly what I had to do. Jasmine's mother, Cindy, moved out and rented a two-bedroom cabin for Jasmine and herself. After Jacob secured the windows and doors, Jasmine moved back home. She tried to get her life back, but most things intimidated her. She went to school only if she had a ride and lived in constant fear of Lyle.

Lyle resurfaced months later. Alyssa, Jasmine, and Jake were fishing at Wilson Lake. Parker planned to meet them as soon as he got off work. He would have been there already, but he got delayed. Jasmine and Alyssa walked to the bathroom, unbeknownst that Lyle had been watching them. When Jake yelled, "Hey, I caught something." Alyssa ran to her brother, leaving Jasmine alone. Lyle made his move; he walked into the multi-stalled room and closed the door. Lyle saw the only stall occupied and waited until Jasmine walked to the sinks to wash her hands. He grabbed Jasmine from behind, sliding his hand inside her pants. Lyle placed his other hand over Jasmine's mouth to quiet her. She felt his erection against her and tried to bite his hand. He ripped open her jeans and exposed himself as the door opened, and Parker walked in. Parker grabbed Lyle and threw him across the room, yelling to Jasmine to get into his truck. Lyle threw the metal trash receptacle at Parker, knocking the wind out of him, and escaped. Parker then dragged himself up using a sink as leverage and followed out the door. He saw Lyle run off into the woods, noticed Jasmine trembling inside his truck, and peered over at the water as Alyssa and Jake ran toward them.

Parker drove the kids back to my house; it took hours to calm Jasmine down. I knew what I had to do. Although I tried to let the authorities take care of it, it was useless. This wasn't a big city; the system was faulty. I knew I needed to take over, and I'm worried because I'm rusty, but this poor child will never be safe unless I do this. Lyle needed to die.

Before beginning surveillance, I reached for the journals. I needed to relive Donovan's torture to gather the strength to summon my dark thoughts, my inner goddess. A headache hammered against my skull as I chose a random journal from the box.

DONOVAN INVITED THE GUY DOWN THE HALL OVER FOR A BEER. We watched Jeopardy on television. I knew to be quiet, yet the answer slipped before either man could. Donovan went off, calling me a dumb "C" word. I'm not dating these entries anymore. Every day is the same, Pain. Torture. Sexual assault. Our neighbor slipped out unnoticed and that's when all hell broke loose. I ruined his night. It started with a backhand across the face. He dragged me into the bedroom and sodomized me. The pain was horrific.

I walk on eggshells all the time. I try to make his favorite meals, but if they are not perfect, there's trouble. Tonight, I made him a steak, and I ate a salad. The steak was overcooked, according to him. He picked it up with a fork and flung it across the kitchen; it landed on the refrigerator and slid down, leaving a greasy trail before landing on the floor. He flipped the table; it landed onto my lap, hot food and the salad landing in a heap on me and around me, littering the kitchen floor. Donovan strutted over to me and hissed, "You are a stupid whore. You can't even cook a decent meal. He pulled my chair from beneath the rubble and kicked me in the chest. The chair landed on its side, my head hitting the tile floor. He slammed the door as he left. I heard a gentle tap on the door. Lisa from across the hall stood there, her mouth open to say something. Instead, she stepped inside and helped me clean the mess.

. . .

ONCE I KNEW LYLE'S ROUTINE, I DECIDED WHEN TO UNLEASH THE beast, my inner goddess. In my mind's eye, I see how I will execute him. I will park my car behind the vacant gas station hidden by the overgrown weeds. Through the woods to the back of his house. The curtains were illuminated, and I noticed shadows pass by the window and knew he was at home. After a week of watching, I decided it would happen in his backyard; he hung out by his fire pit often, drinking and grilling hot dogs on a stick. I waited in the woods; he was later than usual this evening. I'm fidgety, turning my head from side to side, almost compulsively. I'm eyeballing the woods, trying with my mind's eye to see into the shadows of the dense foliage. He came out with a bottle of moonshine in his hands, and I heard him talking to himself. I watched as he cupped his jeans and said, "You got yourself some young poontang tonight." He staggered to his wooden rocker, tried lighting the fire pit, but was too intoxi- cated to do it. After several tries, it lit. While he tended the fire, uncertainty hits, I doubt myself before the bravado appeared. I slipped behind him and struck him with my yard sale sledge- hammer. I was rusty. He felt the searing pain as his jaw cracked, his mouth filled with blood as his lower jaw fell open on one side. Almost as though I had broken a hinge off a door. His knees gave way. He tried to turn, even in his drunken stupor, he knew to move away. He turned toward me, his eyes registered surprise as he snarled. Before he spoke, our eyes locked. His snarl infuriated me. Uncontrollable rage burned in my

gut. I lunged, quickly I jerked my arm to his head. The weapon arced. He moved, and I connected with his face. The hit dragged from the side of his forehead to his nose. Blood spurted from his nose and the gash on the side of his face. He stumbled back, covering his injury with his hands. I staggered with the momentum as I swung again. I hit him on the temple. The cracking sound brought bile to my throat. He staggered and spun away from me, dropping into the bonfire. I needed to be sure he was dead, so I hit him again, in the back of his skull. When the last blow came, the sound of his skull cracking as the fragments pierced his brain. He fell forward into the flames of hell. I almost vomited on top of him. I emptied my stomach at the sound of his bones breaking and the stench of burned hair. The fires of hell have received him. Blood is dripping from the weapon. I hate it, the color, the metallic smell, the gore.

I tossed the note onto a chair. **Menoetius, Titan of Violent Anger, and human mortality. Justice is served.** I'm sick, I'm tired, my breathing is rapid as I make my escape into the woods.

TIRED OF LIVING IN A CAMPER IN THE WOODS, HE RENTED AN apartment. He had identities to choose from, he packed up his belongings and chose Mason Rucker as his new name. He pulled the camper into the back lot of the apartment building on top of the hardware store. The efficiency apartment wasn't much larger than the camper, but it had real plumbing. He'd been in the apartment for years when his 'client' made her move. *She is weakening.* He saw her take down the latest man, but it took longer than other crimes. He wondered about her inner demons. When he observed her killing these men, her face changed. She was almost unrecognizable, as though possessed by evil spirits. When with her family, she was beautiful. Stunning actually, someone he could fall in love with. Her children were nice kids, her husband was a kind man, even the old lady was sweet. It was during those times that he envied Jacob Swanson. By all appearances, he had the perfect family.

I RUSHED BACK TO THE CHURCH AND NOTICED PARKER'S TRUCK parked and rushed down to the office and changed. When I stepped out, Parker waited on the steps. He needed supplies for the evening meeting. I blurted without thinking, "I think Lyle hurt someone."

"What makes you say that Andressa?"

"I overheard him say it!"

"What exactly did he say?"

"He cupped himself and said something about getting some young 'coontang'? What the hell is that?"

"Did he say 'poontang'?"

"Yes, maybe that is what he said," I replied as my cell phone pinged with an incoming text. I peered at the screen; it was from Jacob.

Jacob: Honey, mom is not feeling well, and I must leave right now. A young girl was raped in the park. She is only sixteen. We found Lyle's wallet nearby, and I'm off to make the arrest.

My heart dropped, and I felt the bile rise to my throat, knowing that it would be my husband first on the scene to see what I did. I rushed home, leaving Parker to set up the meeting without me.

I hurried inside, and my mother-in-law struggled to breathe. She'd been dealing with a terrible cold and sounded congested. After placing a call to her doctor, I changed my clothes. I hadn't changed out of my black outfit at the church. I bundled them up in a ball and placed them in a trash bag and threw them in my trunk under the fabric grocery bags I used, where the bloodied murder weapon rested under the liner.

Glory's doctor asked me to take her to the emergency room. I told the kids to lock up and not answer the door and rushed Glory over. I met with Jacob, who had found Lyle's body. They took Glory into an exam room. Jacob walked over to me but didn't reach out to hug or kiss me, which was something he usually did. He grabbed my arm and pulled me into a small consultation room and closed the door. He reached into his pocket and pulled out a small plastic bag and extracted a strand of long brown curly hair. MY HAIR!

"Andi, is this yours?"

I couldn't lie to him; he knew me too well. Groping for an appropriate response I couldn't find one. I took the coward's way out and didn't answer.

"I found it on Lyle's dead body." His question lingered in the air, unanswered. The silence is uncomfortable. I averted my eyes. Jacob knows my tells, I'm fidgety. Before I twist my hands together, I shove them in my jean pockets doubting he'll let this go. I'm afraid I'll reveal my dark secret. My inner dark goddess. The call to justice. Hyper aware of the cool temperature of the hospital, my arms break out in tiny bumps. My mother called it goose flesh. The thoughts in my mind are spinning out of control. I feel my inner goddess is leaving me in a lurch. I don't know what to do. My brows crease and I squint at Jacob, mostly to read him. His bright orbs stared into mine. *Is that disbelief on his face?*

Jacob broke eye contact and diverted his gaze, and mumbled he must check on his mother before getting back to work. He left without a kiss. My thoughts were in a jumble. I knew I couldn't lie. I'd forgotten to pull my hair into a cap, and I couldn't even find my voice. I pulled open the door and hurried toward Glory's room. I walked away from my bewildered husband, in uniform, standing watching me leave.

Jacob checked on his mother, barely speaking to me. He couldn't even look at me. "I've got to get back. I'll see you at midnight." I watched as the love of my life walked away from me, his head down, defeated and confused. My heart raced, and I worried as I watched him. I saw him reach into his pocket, retrieve the plastic bag with the strand of hair and throw it into the trash receptacle, not looking back. They treated Glory for bronchitis and released her later that evening. We got home just as Jacob did. I helped her get comfortable in bed and went into our bedroom.

Jacob sat up under the blankets, reading. I went into our bathroom and noticed a spot of blood on my neck. Damn it, I am rusty! I took a quick shower and changed into my nightgown. Worriedly I went into my bedroom, hoping that Jacob would be asleep. He wasn't. He stood by the bathroom door. "Do you want to tell me what went down tonight?" Jacob's lips were in a thin line, his gaze steady on mine.

"I'm not sure what you mean."

"I'll be more direct. Did you go over to his house? Did you, or do you know who is doing this?"

I shrugged my shoulders, "Jacob, why would I care who is doing this?"

"Because people are getting murdered!" he growled.

"People? You consider them people?"

"What would you call them?"

"Fucking monsters." Jacob's eyes widened, and he stepped back. My use of a foul word shocked him. It was like a fire lit deep in my gut. "You do not know how monstrous these bastards are or were. I lived through it. As a police officer, you only saw a smattering of what I went through." Oh, now the fire raged inside of me. I had to be careful not to slip. I pointed to my top teeth. "See these pearly whites? They're implants. My former mother-in-law paid to have my teeth replaced after her son knocked them out when I was twenty-five years old. I told you a little about what I experienced during Donovan's reign of terror. He locked me in the bedroom, sometimes all day. Without a bathroom, I resorted to using zip-lock bags and jars. I hid protein bars and water." Trembling at the memory, I continued. "Does that not sound monstrous to you?" I wrapped my arms around myself. I couldn't believe I had to justify this to my husband. I never wanted to speak of my terror again, yet here I was reliving the horrors. "Donovan's cruelty was off the chart."

"I get it, Andi. But whoever is doing this needs to stop. It is a crime, a serious crime. Let the police handle it."

I couldn't help myself and I snorted. "The police? Did they help me? No, they didn't. They failed me and many others." I spit. "And that little shit is stirring up the police with his social media posts about his 'father'." I used finger quotes. "Not once does he ask who hurt his mother, who now has a traumatic brain injury and needs constant help." I shook my head. "Not one ounce of help from him, Alan Stevens Junior." My voice echoed my contempt. "The support group helps her. We all cook an extra serving of meals each day and freeze them. We take her to doctor's appointments, clean for her, do her laundry. Keep her company. The support group, not her son." I stepped away. "Please never tell me again that the police have it. It's insulting to me as a victim and to my friends." I turned down my side of the bed, "Jacob, my story is not unique. Abusers do anything they can to break you both physically and mentally. You probably cannot fathom the horrors because you are a good man, a wonderful man. But these men and sometimes women exist and it's hell on earth for their families."

Realizing I probably hurt his feelings, I muttered. "It's not the police department's fault, Jacob, I know this. But the good ole boy mentality of the justice system in this town is really the issue. Women's issues seem to take a back burner with domestic violence. At least it was in my situation."

"Andi, I don't know how to respond." he pointed at me, his eyes blazing. "If you know something, you better speak up, otherwise you could be charged with withholding information in an active investigation."

"Jacob." I sighed, "I just did." I spoke up, just didn't give him what he wanted, and I never would. That last hit took a lot out of me. I'm getting older, I'm weaker, and it took three swings to take him out. I know I need to stop. Yet I'm compelled by forces I cannot control. I climbed into bed next to him, my back to him. We hadn't ever argued, and I wasn't sure how to act. I was fearful of giving away too much. My husband was a police officer, and he knew me better than anyone. I felt him slide down and turn off the lamp. He moved toward me and wrapped his arm around my waist and kissed my shoulder. He whispered. "Did you go to speak with Lyle?" I nodded, taking the lie that just fell into my lap. "Baby, you can't do shit like that. Did he hit you?"

"No, he just pulled me to him by my shirt. He sneered and spewed about me being a weak woman and couldn't tell him anything." The smooth lie fled my mouth as easily as spreading softened butter on toast.

Jacob kissed my neck. "Promise me you won't do anything foolish like that again. I won't survive losing you." He continued touching me and caressing me and turned me onto my back and kissed me. Somehow when Jacob pressed his lips to mine, the world I forged on chaos and death seemed so far away. He reached beneath my nightgown and slid my panties off. He made desperate love to me, almost as though it might be the last time. While my mind was a cacophony of thoughts. *Does he suspect me? Will he think I was the last person to see Lyle alive? What will happen to my family if I'm a suspect and caught. I need to stop. But I can't. The darkness consumes me.*

Nineteen

The news station was on in the kitchen, the volume louder than usual. I stepped into the kitchen where my mother-in-law sat, her gaze transfixed on the television. She mumbled good morning as she listened. **"For the last decade and a half, someone bludgeoned men to death in the sleepy town of Clayton Heights. Police are baffled. They claim the perp is extremely organized, highly capable, and intelligent. Agents want to understand his reasonings, his goals. They are confident, none of this is random, but methodically planned and carried out at the most opportune times."** Glory shook her head and turned the television off. Wheezing, she said, "You be careful sweetheart when you go out at night. Times are simply crazy."

"I will, mom." Her voice sounded weak, her breathing was worsening. We took her back to the hospital.

As spring opened its floral-scented arms to summer, Glory succumbed to pneumonia.

Our family was utterly heartbroken to lose Glory, she was such an integral part of our family. Jacob was in a tailspin as was I to lose 'My Glory.' Although I had a wonderful mother, Glory was equally wonderful. Our strong bond was now severed by death. We were all grieving her loss and would be for a long time. We were blessed to share our lives with such a sweet woman. When she said, "Bless your heart," she meant in from deep within hers.

~

JACOB NEVER BROUGHT UP LYLE AGAIN, BUT HE ALSO STOPPED sharing. If I asked how his day was or where they were in the investigation, he replied with one-word answers. Our foundation of trust seemed cracked, and Jacob looked at me differently. But not Jasmine, she looked at me like I was special.

Every time I saw her, she blossomed. I think she may have suspected something because after the news stations reported Lyle's death, she hugged me and spoke, "You didn't break your promise, and you've kept me safe." Maybe it was just my paranoia.

"I tried honey, but whoever that man was that hit Lyle was the person who ended your fear," I replied.

The migraines intensified and became more frequent as my worries increased. Fear and panic kept me close to home. We socialized with Parker and Rosie and their three girls. But I did little else outside my house. I didn't attend the support group every week, only when I felt strong enough to do so or when they needed me to host. The horrors were too much to listen to each week. My decision to end Jasmine's torment was reckless and not planned out. I feared my husband would put two and two together from the past deaths and connect them to the support group and me.

I had trouble sleeping, vividly remembering Donovan and the abuse. Although I knew Jacob would never hurt me, I didn't want to become a burden or affect his career. He'd applied to become a deputy and rumor had it he would get the promotion.

I adored Jacob more than he could imagine, and I loved our family fiercely. But something was compelling me to retaliate against the horrors of abuse—an uncontrollable drive. I was grateful for the years of relief, but Lyle's violence against Jasmine set me in a tailspin.

A month after Lyle's death, a new member appeared at our meeting, a man, the father of three children. A teenage girl and twin boys who were seven. He drove them to Oklahoma to his parents for safety. His wife had been beating him for years. She was volatile, an alcoholic and mentally ill. She signed herself out of the hospital against medical advice and continued her reign over her husband and children. It appalled me to learn that she sexually abused the boys, and they were in counseling in Oklahoma.

It took several meetings before Daniel shared his story. His nerves were perceptible. "I'm Daniel Krone. I know I'm gonna sound like a wimp, but my wife is abusive. My twin boys are in counseling because she sexually abused them. She pushes me, trips me, and blocks me from leaving the room. I'm a soldier. I know how to fight, but this is my wife. How could this happen to me? He lowered his head. "She calls me names, in front of my team. Can I repeat language here? In church?"

I nod. "Of course, you can be frank here."

"Failure. Loser. Flaccid dick. Pussy." He shook his head. "She stopped me from visiting my family, controls how I dress and spend money. Where I go and who I could talk to. If I break one of her rules, she'll hit, slap, shove, and kick me. Tell me I'm crazy. Threatens the dog, the children and blames me for her behavior, that I deserve it. Using coercive tactics, Rae aimed to dominate me and attack my character. She was a police officer in our old hometown and dangled her power to destroy me professionally. For Christ's sake, I'm a soldier protecting our country, yet I can't protect myself from my wife. It's a dire situation and I'm walking through hell." He nodded, inhaled, and stepped down as his eyes glistened and his face pinked.

I walked by him, squeezed his arm, and stepped behind the podium. "I just wanted to mention something about closure. We hear it from time to time and we've all mentioned at one point or another of needing closure." Taking a breath, I continued, "It's better to let things go. Not to fight for closure, don't chase answers, don't ask for explanations, and don't expect people to understand where you are coming from. You cannot heal a person who keeps using their anger and dissatisfaction as an excuse to hurt you."

"You'll probably get questions from friends or family who have never lived what we lived or live through. Like why doesn't she or he leave?" I nod toward Daniel. "There are several reasons. Because the abuser has us so brainwashed that we believe it's our fault. We believe we can't make it on our own. Because we think we could just try harder, and the abuser will be the person we agreed to marry. We believe our abuser will harm our family. They'll tell the authorities we're terrible parents. Because they control the money and convince us, we can't make it on our own." I sipped water and continued, "The bottom line is that they beat all rationalization out of us. We stayed out of fear."

"I remember the one and only time I tried to run away. I had no money, but when I could, I'd shop at the grocery outlet for cereal and other boxed and more affordable items. I'd use the same empty box from home and just fill it with the cereal I bought for a dollar fifty-nine. I'd save the difference in an envelope and hide it in a tampon box. After a vicious beating, I took the envelope and slipped from the apartment with the backpack I had hidden in the basement laundry room. I got a ride from a neighbor, the same woman who frequently called the police. Lisa took me to the bus station and spotted the difference. She suggested I go to North Carolina instead of New York, thinking he would suspect I went home. Lisa told me a friend lived in Raleigh and would help me out. She even gave me a crisp one-hundred-dollar bill she got for a birthday gift from her parents. I waited in the lot where they parked the buses until departure time. I hid behind them so if he should guess and come, he wouldn't see me. The bus finally opened the door, I took two steps up when I felt myself falling backward. Donovan had reached for the backpack and pulled me down the steps and toward the parking lot. He wrapped his arm around me as though he were my lover, pressing his lips to my ear, as though it was a lover's kiss. Not one person questioned us. Not one person noticed my bruises or my fear or heard his whispered threats. I then realized I was alone, and he would probably kill me at some point."

Twenty

A few weeks later, Daniel returned, his arm in a sling, sporting a black eye, and he mentioned a cracked rib. His face lacked color, and he moved slowly. His wife put a beating on him when he wouldn't tell her where the children were. The police department fired her from the force a few years ago but she still had a gun. She put it to his head during the last disagreement. He was grateful that his parents had downsized prior to him bringing the children, and she didn't know where they lived.

Daniel spoke again that night, and he gave graphic details on what his wife did to the two little boys. He sobbed, and we all cried with him, never having heard of such horrors that a mother could do to her babies. Everyone was fond of him and knew it took great strength to speak. I knew what had to happen. She had to die. It was all I could think about; her death and saving those kids and him. I knew her name, Rae, and which liquor store she frequented. I began my surveillance. It took some time because once she did a liquor run; she didn't leave the house for days. During which Daniel suffered through more beatings. We offered him a safe house, knowing he had to work. He ended up staying with Pastor Robinson and they became buddies. Daniel was there each week and helped me set up for the meeting, cleaned up afterward and walked me to my car where we often had a friendly chat. He was a kind man, and my heart broke for him. I often wondered if Jacob saw us talking and thought there was more to it. There wasn't. He was just a lonely man doing the best he could in a horrific situation.

Almost a month went by when Rae stepped into the store. I followed her inside. I knew it was her from the picture that Daniel showed me and her social media page. She was a mean-spirited person. She almost had the cashier in tears. A week later, I saw her come out of a bar. The same bar where I took down Bart Cruz. She got into a small older Toyota and swerved all over the road. She hit a tree on Henderson Road, a small country road with a few houses spread far apart. I went over to help. She climbed out of the car and told me to leave. I had my trusty weapon behind my back. She knew who I was and said, "What do you want from me?"

"Did you, do it? Did you hurt your little boys?"

"Hurt them? No, I just taught them how to be better lovers, not like their weak ass father."

A headache hammered against my skull. Spots appeared before my eyes and I think I blacked out because the next thing I knew, I held a bloody weapon, and I was sitting in my car. I took off and turned the corner as another car's headlights approached. I made it to the church in record time and followed my routine. By the time I heard the sirens, I was already home and showered. The kids were asleep. I showered and climbed into bed before Jacob returned from work. I pulled my rosary out of my nightstand and prayed, like I did most nights. My old Catholic school trained me well.

The following morning, I read in the newspaper about Rae Krone's death. The killer left a note, one I didn't remember leaving. It read **Tartus, god of the deepest, darkest under-world. Justice is served.**

~

HE TOOK LONGER TO ANSWER, AND WHEN HE DID; HE WAS ABRUPT. "What?" His voice was gruff.

"She took out a woman. Something is wrong. She was almost zombie like."

"I don't need or want your thoughts, just frequent updates." His tone held an edge, a sigh floated through the line, his tone changed. "Do your job, your expenses are being paid, and at the end of this contract, you'll be financially able to retire if that is your desire. See this out."

"All right." He realized he was talking to no one as his boss ended the call.

<h1 style="text-align:center">Twenty-One</h1>

Benjamin Ellington returned and reiterated this is the work of a serial killer, whom they named the 'Mythology Killer.' An irritated man, he despised being back in the small town because there weren't fancy stores to buy designer suits or upscale restaurants. Not even fast food. Just the meals cooked in the B&B and the small local cafe. Not one attractive single woman, apart from Rachel Foss. She was thin and fit and had average sized breasts. Foss was smart and ballsy. She continually annoyed him by insisting the unsub was a woman. She also assumed she was smarter than him.

Additional agents arrived in town, and I was terrified. They interviewed the members of the support group again. They again assigned Jacob to work with them. Little did I know that Rachel Foss was back on the team, older and wiser now. Something about our interactions or when she spotted me in the grocery store unnerved me. Every now and again, she attended the meetings and never took her eyes off me. Fortunately, most liked Jacob, and my interview went well as did all the group members. They saw us as victims and too damaged to hurt anyone. They looked at the family of the deceased and the families of the women they'd abused. Thankfully, they didn't have knowledge of the basement office. I was off the radar. For now.

Our little support group got through several interrogations unscathed. But things unraveled quickly. Something changed in my marriage. Jacob changed after he mentioned Rachel acted indifferently toward him. Almost rude. He became aloof, often watching me when he thought I was unaware. I hated that I caused him to doubt me, hated that I was careless. I tried to act normal and be the same woman I'd always been, but there was something different. She took a dislike to me before, and I'm guessing she is the one who thinks the killer is a woman. Jacob mentioned previously that she did. He no longer shared anything work related with me. Nothing about the investigation. *Did he suspect me? He did!*

I learned from the news that the Division of Criminal Investigation (DCI) was providing expertise, resources and experience in the investigation. They have met with the county Sheriff's office and the FBI in a collaborative effort to search for clues of the serial killer. The investigation was still in its infancy and there was no timeline of how it would progress.

The team pulled records of cell phones that pinged at the scenes; they blocked roads, checked trunks. They speculated the killer was a friend of the family of the abused.

When they came up empty, Benjamin and the team brainstormed. "What we know is this is psychological warfare. The perp is proud of his crimes, displays random acts of anger and distorted views of society. He is emotionally driven to act out of rage. Doesn't believe he is like any other criminal. He is deeply religious and took a devious path of vengeance." He paced as he spoke. "Let's look at local suspects with mental health issues."

The team returned to their computers, except for Rachel. She walked to the front and placed her hands on her hips. "Benjamin keeps referring to the unsub as a man. I'm convinced she's a woman. One hundred percent convinced."

Her eyes bore into Jacob's when Chuck burst through the door. We have another body out on Henderson Road. Chairs screeched across the floor as they flew out the door, up the stairs, and out the back door to the parking lot. Without speaking, three cars pulled up where they found the police tapes marking off the area, a sheet covering the victim. Benjamin nodded to the officer to remove the sheet. They were gob smacked to see a woman. The officer spoke, "Name is Rae Lynn Krone, former San Diego Police." Benjamin's eyebrows raised. "She still had an ID card on her. I called the M.E. already."

Jacob stepped forward and noticed the injury was like the others. Benjamin caught his gaze.

"Thoughts?"

"Same perp." Jacob took photos of the blood drips leading away from the wrecked car. He assumed the perp followed her. The road was paved, and the only tire marks were of the victim's older Toyota.

Later Rachel went to speak with the M.E. Dr. Butterworth, who passed her a sealed plastic bag with scrubs and nodded toward the bathroom. Rachel changed, pulling her hair into a pony and securing it with a clip she kept in her purse and donned the cap. She stepped into the room and Dr. Butterworth uncovered the body. She surveyed the woman's gaping hole in her skull. She was still dressed in her street clothes and reeked of alcohol.

"I spoke to her estranged husband. He's heading back. He has been in Oklahoma visiting his kids. They have cleared him as a suspect?"

"Yes, the local police went to the house. He was tucking the kids into bed. He had receipts for a movie he took the kids to see. As well as a receipt for a local restaurant for dinner." She snickered, "You know, I'm confident I know who this killer is." The men ignored her voice as though it were mere background noise. She was used to it. The misogyny. This town was the worst for the, 'It's a man's world ideology.'

Rachel felt it in her bones that the killer was Andressa Swanson. She wasn't a large woman, but one time she stopped by the house. She was in the pool with the kids, her upper arms were muscular and there wasn't an ounce of fat on her. Her six-pack abs and muscular thighs showed a strict workout routine. Before they left the area almost a decade ago, Rachel followed the young mother several times. She ran track, and during a conversation she learned from Jacob that Andressa worked out in their home gym for stress management and pain relief. He mentioned how she suffered at the hands of her first husband. It all made sense to Rachel. She fit.

Cocky, she headed to the Swanson house and knocked on the door, knowing Jacob was at the station. Andressa responded to the door, surprised to see Agent Foss. "Mrs. Swanson, do you have a minute?"

"Sure, come on in. I'm helping Jake with some math homework."

"I hated math." Trying to put Andressa at ease.

"I enjoyed school. Even math." She rolled her eyes as though admitting her dorkiness. "Would you like something cold to drink, or would you prefer coffee?"

"Nothing, thank you. I have a pop in the car. It's my addiction."

"I enjoy a glass here and there, but we don't keep it in the house. Jacob and I are kinda health nuts." Andressa pointed to the living room and Rachel stepped in and sat on the sofa. Andressa sat in Glory's chair. "What can I do for you, Agent Foss?"

"I wanted to talk to you about Donovan King. That was his name, right? Your first husband?"

"Yes, it was."

"I understand he abused you?"

"It was decades ago. Why do you need to discuss Donovan?"

"Well, he died, right? Leaving you a widow."

"Yes, he died of an overdose. He had massive amounts of narcotics in his system." I admitted. "How is that relevant?" Her face reddened and her brows drew together. Andressa fought for control, not to spew what Donovan did to her.

"It's not really." Agent Foss shook her head and stood, turned and made her way to the front door. She stepped onto the front step and turned toward Andressa. "I know you're the killer." She spits, her breath reeked of contempt. "You wouldn't be the first woman to be knocked around to have had enough to take the law into your own hands. First Mr. King and now a vigilante." Andressa's face remained expressionless. Stoic. She's surprised at how astute the agent was. Disbelief registers on her face, hoping it will convince her how absurd her theory is. She's a smart woman and Andressa was panicking; her greatest fear stood on the porch with an arrogant grin. At one time she was the typical battered woman, afraid to be in her home, which should have been a safe place, but even more afraid to run away. With those words, Agent Foss stepped onto the grass and stepped into her vehicle. A confident grin spread across her face. She waved, the grin not fading. Andressa knew then 'Plan A' must be put into place.

❧

THE OBSERVER SAT IN HIS BEAT-UP CAR WATCHING AS HE OFTEN did. His senses pinged and the agent said something upsetting. He looked at Andressa's face and recognized the panic. All the years of watching, he knew her better than his late wife. He called the boss and didn't wait for the typical, "Yeah or what?"

"I think the FBI is onto her."

"Tell me why." He demanded. He told him everything he saw and what he could hear and the conclusion he came to.

"Okay, your job is done. Go home. Now! I just wired the balance into your account."

Without expressing gratitude, the line went dead. He packed his stuff and went to the airport and bought a ticket home. He left the camper in the parking lot and a note for his landlord, along with the title, telling him to keep it or sell it.

D DAY IS HERE, A DAY I PRAYED WOULDN'T COME. AGENT FOSS knows. It's only a matter of time before the FBI shows up. I feel my heart racing deep in my chest. I have just a few minutes to get out. To save my family. I hurried into my bedroom and rushed into the ensuite. Put the contacts in my eyes, blinked at the discomfort and grabbed the backpack hidden deep in my closet. The backpack I saved in the event the FBI caught me. I cast a glance at my children, tears streaming down my face. Their heads were down, doing homework. My husband is working. I pray as I make my way to the front door. The love a mother has for her children isn't like any other love. I'm leaving to protect them. I must protect them from the fallout of my arrest. I couldn't let them suffer through my capture and trial. What would happen to my family if I'm caught? Convicted? Does anyone really care about the innocent families of those who commit crimes? I slipped unnoticed out the front door. The summer sun heats the macadam as I hurry to the car. Despite its bright rays, all I see is gloom. I'm leaving all that I love behind. I back out of the driveway and leave my neighborhood as tears cloud my vision. Veering right, I headed to the highway, taking the shortcut through Devil's Curve. *Is Devil's Curve this road's actual name, or a moniker made by the town? I hadn't learned the answer in all of my years in Clayton Heights.* I'm weeping for my husband, my children, my aging parents, my brothers. I'd never forgive myself for bringing this into their lives. I love them more than the sun's rays could burn, more than a zillion suns. Tears clouded my vision as I whipped around Devil's Curve. Something slammed into my car, and it careened. I tried to correct the spin. I screamed. Now, of all times, I didn't need to be delayed by a stupid car accident. The air bag exploded into my face, snapping my head back. My nose bled and my face hurt, then everything went black.

Twenty-Two

Several nights before Andressa's conversation with Agent Foss, Pastor Robinson sat in the living room of the pastoral house watching football on the small television. Something he and Daniel did together, but he was visiting his children in Oklahoma for the weekend. He remembered Andressa had brought over cookies the day before. His favorite person really knew how to cook and bake. She often stocked his freezer with microwavable meals. Healthy, but tasty. His heart was failing. He waited for a break in the game and grabbed three oatmeal cookies from the tin. As he turned to leave, he heard a key slide into the back door. He could tell by the shadow that it was Andressa. It was late and she should be home. He stepped into the shadows of the dining area and watched. Dressed in black, she carried a sledgehammer. He could see the glistening blood on the head as she slipped through the kitchen and down the hallway to the basement door. He heard the door to the utility room squeak open. Thirty minutes later, she left, locking the back door behind her. He waited until he heard her car startup and pull from the parking lot.

The small man stepped from the dark dining room and down the hallway, grabbing the huge metal ring of keys and carefully made his way downstairs. He unlocked the room Andressa used as an office.

At once, the scent of cleaning solution hit his nostrils, and he peered into the sink, finding it wet and the smell stronger. He pulled open the utility closet and found the black clothing she wore earlier neatly folded next to a pair of men's running shoes. "Oh Andressa. You poor tortured soul." Pain twinged in his heart. He reached for the clothing and changed into them. Andressa was a few inches taller, and the pants gathered at the elastic around his ankles. He pulled the running shoes onto the floor and slipped his feet inside and rubbed his fingers over them, his grip as firm as it could be with his arthritic hands. He bound them. A searing pain burned his chest, and he felt the weight of the world sitting there. *It couldn't be his favorite person, Andressa. It just couldn't!* He reached for the tool propped up in the corner and gripped it, swinging it a few times, and dropped it into the sink. The old man gripped his chest as the weight of the world sat there. He reached for the old black phone on the desk that sat next to the computer Andressa used to prepare the weekly missiles. The pain grew stronger. He punched the square buttons. 9-1-1, the call connected at once.

"9-1-1 What's your emergency?" Seeing the call came in from the Pastoral house, "Pastor Robinson, are you okay?" Panic filled the young woman's voice. He was a beloved member of their community.

"I did it. It was me. I'm the serial killer." Pastor Robinson fell to the ground, clutching his chest, the phone still in his hands. Before his last breath wheezed from his chest, he heard the sirens.

Seconds later, another call came in, the switchboard logged in an unusual phone number, a cell phone. A male voice, with a thick accent, spoke. "There's been an accident. A woman took a curve and her car careened off a steep ditch. The car is wedged but I cannot make it down to help."

Knowing full well the area he described, she called the rescue team and dispatched whoever wasn't heading to the church. Trembling, the young girl doubled in on herself and muttered, "What in the holy hell is going on tonight?" Unbeknownst to her, three unrelated things happened at the same time within a three-mile radius. Pastor Robinson confessed to being the killer, and the police found him deceased. Rescue workers found a car hanging precariously at Devil's Curve, and a private aircraft took off from a hanger owned by a wealthy businessman.

The rescue workers peered down the embankment of Devil's Curve. Thick trees and foliage littered the area. Dense canopies of branches cluttered the landscape. Unearthed roots weaved through jagged rocks, leading to the rapid water below. Search and rescue were dispatched, along with divers. They attached the safety gear to their waists. Duke, known for his climbing skills, propelled down the cliff to the overturned car. Finding the car severely damaged, he yelled. "The accident fucked up the car; we might need the jaws." The front windshield was missing and there was blood on the fragments. He landed beside the car, careful not to bang into it and knock it from its precarious position. The smell of gas assaulted his nostrils, and he saw spills dripping from the rocks. He carefully stepped toward the broken passenger window. Other than the purse caught on the center gear shift, there was a lot of blood on the deflated airbag and the seat, but no one was inside. He reached for the purse and held it to his chest as he searched the area before climbing back up. He handed the purse to the Sheriff. "I'm guessing it's now a recovery mission. Lots of blood. Driver went through the windshield." He gazed at the rushing waters below. "I doubt they survived; the water is furious."

He turned to the divers, "Gear up, it's a recovery mission." Duke mumbled, "How many people have to die here before they put up a guard rail?" Frustration heated his comment.

The officer opened the purse and pulled out a brown leather wallet. He opened it and paled when he saw the identification. "Holy Mother of Jesus. Andressa Swanson. Jacob's wife." He rushed to his vehicle and pulled the receiver and changed the channel to the secure stations in the sheriff's office. His heart raced and his mouth dried. His brain screamed *Not Andressa, no, not her! This will destroy Jacob. The entire town! We all love her. Such a good soul.*

The divers found a denim jacket with a tear on the side. Inside the pocket was a package of gum, a soaked tissue and a tube of tinted lip moisturizer.

Once they pulled the car onto the road, forensics found blue thread on the windshield. It matched the jacket found.

Within minutes after pulling the car to land, Jacob arrived. He tried to climb down the rocky edge to help the divers. He screamed her name. "ANDRESSA!" Tears blurred his vision as he brought his hands to his head, falling to his knees.

The Sheriff reached for him. "Son, let them do their jobs."

"She's strong. She could probably climb out. Maybe she's passed out on a rock. Please let me help?"

"We checked the area, Jacob. Duke was the first down there. You know Duke. He would have found her if she were there." The Sheriff turned his head as his eyes watered. To watch Jacob's breakdown was shattering. Jacob dropped to his knees and repeated her name over and over. "Andi, please, let it not be you. I can't live without you. Our kids, this will kill them. She was so good with them, never raised her voice. She was an amazing wife too." Agent Foss squatted next to him, rubbing his back. She felt guilty for terrorizing Andressa, especially more so because maybe their conversation had Andressa driving while upset and scared. She never intended to bring her to justice because she did this town a favor. Her own mother was abused and wished she had the courage back then to take care of the abuser. She merely wanted the self-satisfaction of saying she caught the 'Mythology Killer.' She never intended to tell that dumbass, misogynist Ellingson. Knowing her thoughts were morally gray in this situation, the guilt she felt was over Andressa's death and Jacob's gut-wrenching grief.

The divers surfaced. "Sheriff, we must check again tomorrow. The current is brutal. We have divers downstream too. Perhaps it won't be as bad."

Jacob stood, "I'll dive, I'll look for her."

"No, Jacob, you won't. You are not a professional diver. They are. You are also a father. You have two kids that need you."

"No, they need their mother!" He yelled, "She is their everything, my everything."

After divers checked the local waterways hoping Andressa's body would surface, when it hadn't, Jacob isolated himself and his children. They took a trip to New York to see their grandparents, where they held a memorial service. He would have another in Texas once they found a new pastor. For now, the church was still a crime scene.

CHAOS. THE ONLY WORD THAT COULD DESCRIBE THE NIGHT THAT changed the town forever. Andressa Swanson was missing and presumed dead by the treacherous waters beneath Devil's Curve. Their beloved pastor, Ezekiel Robinson, admitted to being the serial killer who will be forever known as the Mythology Killer. The women of Clayton Heights were grateful as the small man who led them in their path to Godliness was also the man who took out the trash so abusers wouldn't terrorize them.

The murders were incomprehensible to many of pastor Robinson's followers. Such a gentle man of small stature couldn't have to power to do such horrible things. Yet, he had. The FBI closed the case, and they returned to Quantico.

Slowly, the small town returned to a new semblance of normal. Without a Pastor and their beloved Andressa.

~

JACOB WAS DESPONDENT AND FULL OF ANGUISH. ANDRESSA'S LIFE insurance policy afforded

the time to take off from work, to help his children through their agonizing grief. Since they hadn't yet hired a new pastor, the town came together and hosted an emotional memorial service for their beloved friend. Jacob and the children sat in the first row. Jacob could barely lift his head at the beautiful picture displayed at the altar. It was one he hadn't seen before. Her smile was wide, her eyes shining, a candid shot of her beautiful face. The face he loved. He planned to hang this one above the fireplace so his children would see their mother's face every day. Andi looked so happy in the shot, a beaming smile and her vibrant emerald eyes. Her dark hair glistened in the sunlight. It came to him; they took it at Parker's party, years ago. She had changed little over the years, maybe a few lines around her eyes, but she aged gracefully. Days later, he found the courage to go through Andressa's closet and found journals for their children. It was almost as though she expected to die young. For him, she left a letter. He tore it open.

IN HER FAMILIAR SCRIPT, HE READ.

MY DEAREST JACOB,

. . .

If you are reading this, I'm gone. I'm writing not to make you upset but to tell you how much our marriage, you and our children, meant to me. I was happiest in your arms and hope I was a good wife to you, because you were everything to me. Your hands always brought me comfort and pleasure, never pain. I felt safe when you wrapped your arms around me. Your gentle ways taught me how to love and feel loved and worthy. It was you who saved me, your love. You gave me a safe place. I remember that time when I ironed your shirt and burned it. I was crying and before you comforted me, you laid the iron on the other side to burn a matching spot. You made me laugh through my tears that day, and you filled my life with laughter every day.

Just know that I'll be your guardian angel and will be beside you to protect you and our children.

I love you, Jacob. I will forever. Be happy, my darling.

Until we meet again your wife,
  Andi
  XXXO

Sobbing, Jacob carefully folded the paper, knowing he would need to re-read it throughout his lifetime. He plopped into the soft chair Andressa sat in to read when she needed quiet, the same chair where she sat to put on her shoes, his memories so vivid it was like she was there. Her scent was still present. The divers haven't recovered her body yet. He hopes every day she'll walk through the door, or he'll wake to learn it was just a horrible nightmare. Anguished, Jacob stepped into his sneakers to run off the pain. Just like his Andi. He could hear her voice in his mind. "Be happy, darling." But how could he be when his world crashed around him with her loss? He never expected to be a widower this soon. It wasn't fair, she was too young. He gazed toward the sky as he ran. "Andi, I got your letter. I love you too. So much, I feel like I'm dying inside without you." He huffed and ran faster, feeling one with his love. "Andi, the kids, me, we're struggling. I guess that's the price we pay for loving so deeply. How do I do this without you?" He ran a few miles before he reached up to his head, grabbed a fistful of his damp hair, and screamed a word he rarely used, if ever. "Fuck!" A guttural sound as he collapsed on the track and sobbed. It was Parker who found him and sat next to him and rubbed his back. Wordlessly they sat, tears streaming as the sun shined brightly until Jacob could speak. He whispered her name like a prayer.

The Clayton Heights Times
Friday, October 29, 2007

Breaking News
The latest local News
-James Nilson

OUR SMALL TOWN HAS EXPERIENCED TRAGEDIES OF astronomical proportions. Pastor Ezekiel Robinson admitted to being the Mythology Serial Killer, and shortly after succumbed to a massive cardiac event. The police found him deceased on the church's basement floor, the phone still in his hand. Andressa Swanson suffered a car accident at Devil's Curve and is missing and presumed dead.

The townspeople grieve both deaths, leaving our small town devastated. Andressa was a well-loved member of the town, often giving of her time to the church and the abuse support group that met weekly in the Bible study room. The members will continue the meeting and have requested a grief counselor to join them.

Epilogue

The private aircraft took off from a private airstrip miles outside of Clayton Heights. The cloudless sky promised an easy flight. Four men sat in the soft beige leather chairs with a bottle of whiskey and four high ball glasses. They guzzled the amber liquid after clinking glasses. The plane lurched. It dipped with turbulence. After the second shot, the shortest of the men asked, "Who is in the bedroom, amigo?"

He shrugged his shoulders, "Precious cargo, I'm told." He was thankful the passenger slept through the hum and rumbling engines.

Hours later, the aircraft landed on an airstrip nestled on private property in Columbia. Acres upon acres of poppy plants grew surrounding the airstrip. The soldiers rouse the passenger. "Put this on." They tossed a rough hood to the passenger. Their orders were to deliver the guest to the private residence. After what felt like hours, the entourage arrived at the beachside villa. Someone removed the hood, and two men escorted the passenger inside the large home. The passenger noted the thick ceiling fan paddles shaped like palm fronds as they guided the guest to a room on the right. Standing straight and tall as the man on the left knocked. The other two stood guard at the door.

"Enter." The deep baritone, somewhat familiar voice comes from inside.

They stepped inside, ushering the guest into the room. Stepping back, they closed the door behind them. "Welcome to Cartagena. I learned you were in trouble Sis. Are you here to stay?" Alejandro sat; his leg crossed, his ankle resting it on his knee. The scent of cigar smoke lingered in the air.

She lowered her gaze and nodded. "How did I get here?"

"My soldiers were watching over you, Savannah. For years now." The name rolled off his tongue easily.

"Me? Why?"

"To keep you safe."

Alejandro gazed into her eyes. "You can remove the contact lenses now. Your eyes are bloodshot."

She nodded, reached into her right eye, and pinched the lower part of the brown contact lens, then repeated with the left eye.

He nodded toward the gold metal ashtray that held the butts of his favorite cigar. She dropped them among the ashes. Tearful bright green eyes stared back at him. Andressa's eyes.

The End

Author's Note

Dearest friends,

This was a challenging story to write. It took me years to finish it because of learning how horrid abusers could be and Andressa became so real to me. Andressa's story is typical regarding abuse. Many of the instances depicted in this story are real and come from years of research and interviews. How Andressa handled it is purely fictional and should **not** be imitated. Andressa is a figment of my overactive imagination, and she is not based on me, anyone in my family, nor my friends.

Domestic abuse isn't always physical, it's mental, too. Name-calling, shaming, derogatory remarks, threats and other more subtle ways to control another person's thinking are abusive. This form of abuse is disturbing because they aim it at destroying self-esteem and confidence. It undermines a personal sense of reality or competence. Domestic violence must stop.

Each time I worked on this story, it left me in an awful place. Learning the depths of what some people have suffered broke me. I'm so grateful for my amazing husband, who had the patience of a saint when I was snippy, or perhaps downright rude while I worked on this story. He gets me, always has.

My heart goes out to anyone who is or was a victim. Know that there is help out there. It also surprised me to learn that men are victims too.

Much Love,
    Lucia
    XXXO

Goddess of Revenge Playlist

Girl On Fire Alicia Keys
Love Is A Battlefield Pat Benatar
I Will Survive Gloria Gaynor
Vendetta Unsecret
Knocking On Heavens Door RAIGN
Church Lawless
Down to Nothing Brooke Moriber
I'm Not Okay Citizen Soldier
Call Me Shinedown

Domestic Abuse Hotline

1-800-799-7233

Also by Lucia Catherine

The Haunted Hearts Trilogy

Forgotten Identity Book One

On a dark road in South Carolina, a New Jersey housewife's minivan hits a patch of sand and crashes into a tree, leaving her unconscious. When she awakens, she is surrounded by strangers thousands of miles away. Yet, she is a stranger, even to herself. Her memory is gone, and the man who claims to be her father, a famous physician, tells her she is his beloved daughter, Susan Kline.

Recovering in the Beverly Hills mansion, Susan tries to trigger a memory or recognition of the people caring for her. Only to be left with the haunting feeling that she is not who they say she is.

Scars prove she may have a family but forges a life with the man who claims to be her father.

Her path is chosen, her memories gone. Will the past dictate her future?

~

Songbird Book Two

Soon after her high school graduation, a teenage girl from a prominent family disappears. At once, she learns being on her own is dangerous. After facing unbelievable hardships and overwhelming trials, she changes her life, her name, and turns her back on everyone but her newfound community. After decades of living as a ghost, hiding from the real world, and letting her family believe she was dead, she leaves on a quest for help from the woman who assumed her identity and inherited the fortune meant for her.

~

Fallen Apple Book Three

Chelsea Burton leads an investigation into a string of mysterious sexual assault cases. A former victim of sexual abuse herself, she is determined to catch the ferocious mad man who brutally raped and murdered young women in a sleepy town in Tennessee.

Determined to solve the case, Chelsea, along with the Medical Examiner, Tyler Anderson, and her partner Steve, teamed up.

The hunt for the killer lures Chelsea out of her jurisdiction and affects her in dangerous ways. Chelsea discovers someone close to her is keeping dangerous secrets.

And just when everything appears momentarily under control, the case takes a terrifying turn, putting their entire group of friends in danger. Chelsea must make a choice she never dreamed she'd face.

Wanderlust

Author Chase Cornell has just celebrated his second bestseller, and he bought a house on the beach. His career is on an upswing, his dreams are coming true, and he is content. He has sworn off relationships as he loves living life as a bachelor. Until he meets a beautiful woman at the local pub and sparks fly. A professional photographer with a few books of her own, Erica is used to living life without strings.

Disillusioned with her dating life, Erica Wilson walks into her favorite pub and encounters Chase. An enigmatic stranger who ignites in her an unexpected passion that is all-consuming. Like-minded about relationships, they agree on a friends-with-benefits relationship.

Strong, sexy, and fun, Chase is everything Erica didn't know she wanted in a man. Love blooms and when tragedy strikes, Chase's life is torn apart. Erica steps up to help him, uprooting her life when they are thrust into a tumultuous and strained relationship. Neither let their walls down to see what's right in front of them.

❧

The Letter

Angela Rossi couldn't have known how much her life would change when she met the handsome and charming Drew Ward. She couldn't have known she'd fall instantly in love only to learn Drew held a secret that broke her heart just as she discovered she was pregnant.

Drew had never felt for anyone what he felt for Angela. He knew at once she was to be his for the rest of their lives. His heart was shattered by that one phone call on a cold winter day.

Terrified by a stalker, Angela is forced to move hundreds of miles away from home, she arrives at the ranch Drew's mother owns only to learn he isn't there.

Will Drew get there in time to save Angela, or will her stalker find her first?

Follow Me

Please follow me on Facebook: https://www.facebook.com/LuciaCatherineAuthor

Instagram: https://www.instagram.com/authorluciacatherine/

Twitter: https://twitter.com/LuciaKen

Amazon: https://amazon.com/author/luciacatherine

Website: www.LuciaCatherine.com

TikTok: @LuciaCatherineAuthor

www.ingramcontent.com/pod-product-compliance
Lightning Source LLC
Chambersburg PA
CBHW031559310726
48974CB00003B/728